black
dogs

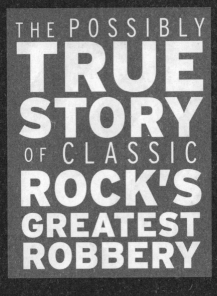

THE POSSIBLY
TRUE
STORY
OF CLASSIC
ROCK'S
GREATEST
ROBBERY

black dogs

JASON
BUHRMESTER

THREE RIVERS PRESS
NEW YORK

COPYRIGHT © 2009 BY JASON BUHRMESTER

PUBLISHED IN THE UNITED STATES BY THREE RIVERS PRESS, AN
IMPRINT OF THE CROWN PUBLISHING GROUP, A DIVISION OF RANDOM
HOUSE, INC., NEW YORK.
WWW.CROWNPUBLISHING.COM

THREE RIVERS PRESS AND THE TUGBOAT DESIGN ARE REGISTERED
TRADEMARKS OF RANDOM HOUSE, INC.

LIBRARY OF CONGRESS CATALOGING-IN-PUBLICATION DATA

BUHRMESTER, JASON,
BLACK DOGS / JASON BUHRMESTER.—1ST ED.
P.   CM.
1. LED ZEPPELIN (MUSICAL GROUP)—FICTION   2. MUSICIANS—CRIMES
AGAINST—FICTION.   3. TAXICAB DRIVERS—FICTION.
I. TITLE.
PS3602.B36B57 2009
813'.6—dc22
2008050094

ISBN 978-0-307-45181-1

PRINTED IN THE UNITED STATES OF AMERICA

DESIGN BY MARIA ELIAS

10 9 8 7 6 5 4 3 2 1

FIRST EDITION

For Mom. You would have laughed the hardest.

contents

ONE

baltimore, maryland

JULY 20, 1973

the albums FLIPPED FORWARD
INTO MY HAND.

Paranoid

Volume 4

Master of Reality

And of course *Black Sabbath*, the album that started it all for
the greatest band in the world: Black Sabbath.

I pulled a copy of each one, stuffed them under my arm and
looked around the Record Barn. I'd been coming here since I
was a kid. In high school I used to sneak into the kitchen in the

middle of the night to make a lunch just so I could pocket my lunch money. By the end of the week I had enough for a few singles.

Not much had changed at the Barn in the months since I had split town. Faded posters covered the grimy front windows, keeping the store dim even in the middle of the afternoon. The stench of pot still hid behind a thin wall of incense, and boxes of T-shirts and albums littered the narrow aisles like always. The owner, Bob, a frizzy-haired David Crosby look-alike, wandered around squeezing more albums into cluttered bins. He stopped in the aisle and stared at me.

"Aren't you supposed to be in school?" he growled.

"I graduated two years ago, Bob," I told him without looking up from the row of records I flipped through.

"Oh," he grunted. "Well, do you need anything?"

He didn't really sound interested in helping me.

"Nah. Just waiting for Frenchy . . . uh . . . Pete."

A few minutes later Frenchy stumbled from the back room. His arms waved wildly around his head and shaggy brown hair swirled around his face. He flung a pile of records on the counter and wiped his face with the front of his Flamin' Groovies T-shirt.

"What the hell's wrong with you, Frenchy?"

"I got caught in a spiderweb in the basement," he said. He patted down his hair then looked up at me. "And don't call me that."

We'd been calling him Frenchy since a night he passed out drunk in the backseat of my car talking gibberish that we decided sounded like French. After I left town he convinced everyone to call him Pete again. It was going to take some getting used to.

"So did Alex actually get out today?" I asked.

"Yeah. His mom's having a party for him tonight."

Frenchy sighed heavily.

"You sure he wants to see you?"

"Probably not," I answered.

Bob disappeared into the back room. I followed Frenchy while he walked through the store. Now and then he stopped to file a record into a bin.

"Man, I shouldn't have told you he was getting out," Frenchy moaned. He moaned a lot.

"I just need to talk to him."

"He didn't answer any of your letters. Why would he talk to you now?"

"I know Alex better than he knows himself."

"You drove all the way down from New York City just to talk to him?"

"Something like that."

Bob returned from the back room with a set of BMW keys in his hand and a briefcase with a Grateful Dead sticker on the side. Something about an old hippie with a BMW and a briefcase made me smile.

"Be sure to lock up, Pete."

"Okay, Bob. See you tomorrow," Frenchy said as the front door rattled closed.

Music played in the store. Something loud and noisy. I liked it.

"Who's this?" I asked.

"The Stooges. They're from Detroit."

"I dig it."

"Really? You actually like something other than Black Sabbath?"

"Just need something to fill the time until their next album."

"Whatever." Frenchy laughed.

"How's your band going?" I asked.

"Which one?"

When he wasn't working at the Record Barn, Frenchy combined his musical talents and marginal high school acting experience into a couple of cover bands that played bars and private events. Want the Rolling Stones to rock your wedding reception? Frenchy can do a hell of a Mick Jagger. Need Neil Diamond at your office holiday party? Frenchy's version of "Sweet Caroline" could get the accounting department on their feet. He could imitate anyone.

Frenchy finished restocking the bins then locked the front door. The cash register chimed as he stabbed at buttons until the drawer shot open. Frenchy grabbed the tray of cash and headed toward the back office. I followed him until he stopped, blocking the doorway.

"Where do you think you're going?"

"I don't know." I shrugged. "Just following you."

"No way. Wait out here."

"What's the big deal? You're just counting out the cash register. I can hang out for that."

"Not a chance, dude. That's my rule. You, Alex and Keith aren't coming near the cash or the safe or the back room. I don't even want you guys near the fucking mop closet. Just wait out there."

I sat on the counter, started to read an issue of *Rolling Stone*, got bored and read *Creem* instead. A flier on bright yellow paper hung on the side of the counter.

THE MISTY MOUNTAIN HOPPERS
LED ZEPPELIN FAN CLUB
MEETINGS EVERY FRIDAY—CALL FOR INFO

I tore it down, folded it up then slipped it into my pocket. A switch flipped from the back room and the lights shut off.

Frenchy reappeared and stood in the middle of the store going over everything in his head to make sure he hadn't forgotten anything. He double-checked the back door then the tiny safe in the office. Then he checked the back door again.

"We need to pick Keith up from work," Frenchy said, turning off the rest of the lights in the store.

"Is he still working at Mancini's?"

"Yeah. Installing car stereos."

"And then uninstalling them in the middle of the night?"

"Of course."

Frenchy fished for his keys then stopped at the front door and turned around.

"Don't you already own those?" he asked, pointing to the stack of Sabbath albums under my arm.

"Wore them out. I need new copies."

"You gonna pay for 'em?"

"What do you think?"

Frenchy sighed and opened the door. We walked together across the empty parking lot as the sun set behind the Record Barn, and Baltimore looked every bit as small as it did when I'd left.

TWO

a payday
of sorts

tony mancini USED THE FANCY-ASS SPELLING OF THE SOUND SHOPPE TO ATTRACT FEDERAL HILL SUCKERS WHO THOUGHT THE STORE MUST BE EUROPEAN. IT WASN'T BUT THE PLOY WORKED ANYWAY. THE GLASS SHOWROOM, LOADED WITH HIGH-END HOME AND CAR STEREO GEAR, ATTRACTED RICH BOYS WHO STOOD AROUND THEIR CAMAROS ARGUING ABOUT EIGHT-TRACK PLAYERS, WHILE INSIDE A DENTIST BLEW A GRAND ON AN ONKYO RECEIVER AND A SONY SUPERSCOPE CASSETTE DECK FOR BLASTING HIS TONY ORLANDO AND DAWN ALBUMS.

Mancini's office sat just to the left of the $700 Celestion Ditton 44 speakers, through a door marked DO NOT ENTER and down a dingy hallway cluttered with boxes, stereo equipment, empty food cartons, porno mags and other garbage. While the salesmen on the showroom floor kissed up to the rich assholes who shopped there, Mancini lurked in his office plotting ways to fuck those customers over. If you were ripped off or screwed over in our town it was the work of Mancini.

Mancini's main operation was Westside Limo, a local car service that drove people to the airport. When Mancini's driver picked you up he checked out your house then he kicked in with the small talk. *Where are you going? I hear it's nice this time of year. Getting away for a few days with the wife, eh?* You sat in the backseat wondering if the driver was a nice guy or just some jerk working you for a bigger tip.

The truth was he didn't give a shit about a tip. By the time the driver pulled up at the terminal you'd told him where you were going, how long you'd be gone, who was staying at your place. Everything but where you hid the jewelry. The driver gave the details to Mancini. While you were eating peanuts on the plane, me and Alex were climbing in your bedroom window to steal back that Onkyo receiver and Sony cassette deck you just bought. Plus, anything else we could find.

Keith started working for Mancini back in high school. He'd been stealing car stereos since the day he figured out you could break a window with the porcelain tip of a spark plug and not make a sound. He really took to it and terrorized every neighborhood, car dealership, church parking lot, anything. Nothing stopped him. He could strip a tape deck from a Dodge Charger right in the high school parking lot during lunch break and still have time to eat and sneak back out for a smoke.

When Mancini's guys installed a new stereo in a car, they slipped Keith the invoice. Keith dropped by the address in the middle of the night, ripped out the system and brought it to Mancini, who put everything back in boxes and sold it again, often to the same idiot who bought it the first time. Keith got a cut. Eventually Mancini hired Keith to work at the Sound Shoppe installing car stereos. That way, your new system was installed and stolen by the same technician. Keith did both jobs well.

Now we were waiting at the Sound Shoppe for Mancini to pay Keith. He always kept us waiting. Keith had met us in the garage, still wearing his greasy coveralls. He hugged me and, after some small talk, led us back to Mancini's office. He yawned and stretched out in a brown metal chair with his arms folded across his chest. He was no criminal mastermind. That's for sure. He went along with whatever put money in his pocket so he didn't have to get a real job. And it didn't take much to keep Keith in business—just enough for beer, cigarettes and comic books.

He certainly didn't spend the cash on clothes. Keith's wardrobe came in three settings: ripped jeans and Stones T-shirt, ripped jeans and Black Sabbath T-shirt or ripped jeans and no shirt. His greasy hair hung in his face. I leaned forward to ask Keith a question.

"Hey. Is that toolbox out there the one we stole from Eastside Auto?"

Keith grinned, showing off the brown edge of a chipped front tooth, the result of a shot he took from a baseball bat in a brawl outside a party one night.

"Yeah," he said. "That's the one."

The tool chest was one of my dumbest ideas ever. It was last summer and Keith needed help getting into Eastside Auto Repair to rip a stereo from a Trans Am that was supposed to be parked inside. When it wasn't there, Alex and Keith wanted to forget everything, but I figured after all of the trouble of getting inside, we had to take something. I decided that we should take the tool cabinet. A giant Snap-on chest that size loaded with gear was worth thousands. It also weighed close to a ton. Mechanics used tow trucks to move them from one garage to another.

We wound up pushing my bright idea twelve blocks in the summer heat. The July weather hit ninety that day, and even though the night air was cool, hot tar from the street pulled against the wheels. We had started on the sidewalk, rolling past the run-down row houses and corner bars, but the rattling toolbox clattered over every crack. We didn't need the attention so I moved us into the dark street. Pushing up the middle of the road doubled our odds of being busted so me and Alex scanned for an escape route every time we saw headlights. We knew the rules, off the street, through the backyards. It went without saying that if we had to run, Keith was on his own.

He wouldn't have made it far. While me and Alex pushed, Keith staggered alongside the cabinet, guiding it up the street. Sweat raced down his bare chest; his neck and arms were beet red with sunburn, and a faded black T-shirt, dotted with cigarette burns, swung from the back pocket of his jeans. His hair dangled close to a cigarette with a long black ash and his eyes were stoned and puffy. At one point, he coughed up a belch, made a face from the taste of stale beer, and swallowed.

He finally forced us to stop at a Laundromat on Jackson Street so he could break in and buy a soda from a vending machine. When he realized that he didn't have any change, we pried open the machine. Once we were inside, I decided we might as well clean out the rest of the machines. Keith wandered around in the glow of the neon sign outside and used a pry bar to knock the change boxes off every dryer and washing machine. We dumped the coins in a cardboard box, set it on top of the tool chest and rolled all the way up Fort Avenue to Keith's house. We sold the tools to Mancini and made more money than we would have with the stereo from the Trans Am.

Keith thought for a minute. He dug a line of dirt and grease from underneath a fingernail. Finally he spoke up.

"When was the last time you talked to Alex, anyway?" he asked.

"The night he got arrested, I guess."

Keith nodded.

"You talked to Danny?"

I glared at Keith. He knew I hated Alex's uncle Danny.

"Can we swing by my place before Alex's party?" he asked.
"I need to shower."

"Since when do you shower?" Frenchy asked.

Keith ignored him.

"That's all the way across town," I said.

"I'll give you five bucks for gas."

Keith was always broke.

"You don't have five bucks."

"I just gotta get it from Mancini. I'll have it in a minute.
You know that. Come on."

"We'll see."

Just then Mancini barged in. He threw open the door and
stopped. He held a box under one arm and stood leaning in
the doorway with his back to us as he yelled at the Mexicans
working behind him in the garage.

"And put those Delco speakers in the Olds not the fucking
Pioneers! I don't care if he paid for them. He ain't fucking
getting 'em."

Mancini looked like a three-hundred-pound caveman. His
nose and mouth sloped down from his face and, his thick black
eyebrows jutted low over his eyes. He left his purple dress
shirt unbuttoned to the middle of his chest and thick black
chest hair sprung through the opening. The shirttail hung out
the back of his stained black dress pants. The entire outfit
probably hadn't been washed in a month. He wheezed as he
trudged across the office then slammed down into the chair
behind his desk.

"Fellas! How have you been?"

He always shouted. Keith and Frenchy muttered something. I stared at the floor.

"What's been going on?"

This was Mancini's rap. He liked to hear the latest gossip and keep tabs on where everyone in town hung out and who had a beef with who. If he knew where you hung out it was that much easier to find you if you fucked him over. And if he knew who your enemies were, it was that much easier to find someone to do the job.

"So how's New York, Patrick?"

"It's good."

"Yeah?" He smirked.

He looked over at Keith like they were both in on the same joke.

"You still working that catering gig with my brother Carmine?"

"Yeah," I said, nodding. "Carmine's a good guy."

Mancini rolled his eyes.

"No, he's not. He's a fucking scumbag but I'm glad you two are getting along."

Mancini opened a thick black binder. The papers inside were loose and stained at the edges with coffee. He smoked and flipped through the papers. He found a pink invoice and squinted at it.

"All right, Keith. That asshole Pannazzo kid installed a new Panasonic deck in the Cutlass his parents bought him last month for graduation. You know where he lives?"

"Yeah. On Juniper."

"Great. Let's get that back. And whatever happened with that Huffman kid I asked you about? He has an eight-track player and a pair of Pioneer speakers in that Trans Am."

"He's been parking in his garage every night. I can't get to it."

Mancini looked up. His eyes were dark and heavy, and when I realized how bloodshot they were, mine began to water. He jabbed at Keith with his cigarette as he sputtered.

"So what! So you break into the fucking garage."

No way was Keith breaking into Huffman's garage. Huffman's old man was a maniac and he kept a pit bull named Peaches locked in the garage. Keith put up a good front, though. He glanced down at the tile and nodded his head then took a drag on his cigarette. He wanted to make it look like he'd thought it over and come to a decision.

"Okay. I'll get it."

Mancini stared at Keith and the room went quiet. The sounds of Spanish music and laughter cut through Mancini's cheap office.

"What the fuck are they doing out there?" Mancini mumbled. He opened the door leading to the garage. The music from the garage shook the shelves in the office.

"Turn that shit down, you assholes, or I'll have every fucking one of you deported!" Mancini screamed. He coughed violently. "You hear me, amigo?"

He slammed the door and sat back down. He and Keith went over the rest of the list. There was a VW Bug that belonged to a girl we went to school with and a new van owned by one of Keith's neighbors. The husband brought it in to Mancini to set up with JBL speakers, a subwoofer and a Pioneer eight-track. Mancini wanted it all back.

"Oh—and I wanted to grab that money from you for last time," Keith said. Whenever Keith asked Mancini for money he made it sound like the thought had just occurred to him even though he and Mancini both knew it was coming. He used to follow this approach with "Is that cool?" but realized it left things open for Mancini's bullshit so he dropped that part.

"What do I owe you again? One-fifty?"

Mancini scrunched up his face and flipped through his binder.

"No. It was three hundred," Keith said.

"If you say so," Mancini said.

He tried to sound like he didn't believe Keith. He wanted to play it off like he was being taken advantage of. He knew how much he owed Keith. No one ripped off Mancini that easily.

He cracked a safe under his desk, pulled out a silver gun, a shoe box wrapped in duct tape and a large folder and placed them on the desk. Then he sat bent over counting money where we couldn't see. He handed the cash to Keith, who stuffed the money in his pocket without counting it, and we bolted from the office and down the empty hallway.

"What do you say, man?" Keith said, climbing into the front seat of my car. "Can we swing by my place first?"

"You got five bucks?"

"Shit." He grinned. He pulled the wad of cash from his front pocket. "Take ten."

I wasn't happy about it but didn't feel like arguing. It was too hot. I stuffed the ten into my pocket. The car struggled in the heat before the engine kicked over with a blast of sweltering air in our faces. Sabbath thundered from the speakers. The car was a piece of shit, but thanks to Keith the stereo sounded fucking great.

THREE

let's spend the night together

the first TIME I MET EMILY WAS IN KEITH'S KITCHEN. IT WAS LAST YEAR AND KEITH'S CHRISTMAS PARTY WAS STUMBLING TO AN END. TWO OF KEITH'S COWORKERS SAT ON THE FLOOR IN FRONT OF THE COUCH PASSING A JOINT AND STARING AT THE CHRISTMAS TREE, WHICH LAY ON ITS SIDE IN THE MIDDLE OF THE LIVING ROOM. A *MISSION: IMPOSSIBLE* RERUN BLARED FROM THE TV AND GIGGLING CAME FROM A BEDROOM UPSTAIRS. KEITH SLUMPED OVER THE KITCHEN TABLE WITH HIS HEAD DOWN, A WARM BEER IN HIS HAND. I WOBBLED ACROSS THE KITCHEN AND CRUNCHED ACROSS A BAG OF POTATO CHIPS ON THE FLOOR. ALEX FOUND ME BENT OVER IN THE FRIDGE DIGGING FOR ANOTHER BEER.

"These girls want to get out of here. Can we give them a ride?"

I shut the door and tried to stand upright, swaying a bit. Alex leaned in the doorway. Two girls, a blonde and a brunette, whispered to each other behind him.

"We sure can," I said. "Let's go."

We piled into my car. Tina's blond hair, blown out Farrah Fawcett–style, bobbed in the back window as she talked loudly with Alex. Emily sat up front playing with her straight black hair and didn't say anything until Tina teased her about being shy. She turned back and told Tina to fuck off then grinned a bit before turning back to stare out the window. She was young and gawky, all legs, in giant platform sandals and tiny denim shorts. She opened the glove box and dug through a pile of eight-track tapes.

"*Black Sabbath. Paranoid. Master of Reality.* Do you have anything other than Black Sabbath?"

"Not really," I answered.

"That's pretty weird."

"I like Sabbath. What's weird about that?"

"Are you some kind of satanist?" She grinned. "You're not going to sacrifice us, are you?"

"Nope. We only sacrifice virgins," I joked. She laughed loudly and fidgeted with the radio dial. She stopped when she heard "Goodbye Yellow Brick Road" playing on WKTK.

We drove to Tina's house in Roland Park, winding down tree-lined roads near the Baltimore Country Club. I'd only been to this part of Baltimore once. It was a night me and Alex drove around casing houses, looking for one set up to rob. A suspicious cop pulled us over but let us go. After that, we decided the area was too risky and never came back.

I turned off the lights as we pulled up along a low rock wall outside Tina's house. Alex and I lingered back by the car as the girls stumbled across the manicured lawn. We weren't sure what to do. These situations were like special forces operations. Me and Alex had crawled in bedroom windows, crept up stairs and even used ladders to help chicks escape from their parents. Emily and Tina opened the front door.

"Get in here before the neighbors see you," Tina whispered from the front step.

Tina's parents were out of town. They had driven to Florida with her brothers for Christmas while Tina finished school.

Tina's grandfather was dropping her at the airport tomorrow to fly down and meet up with the rest of her family. Emily was spending the night.

Our tactics changed once me and Alex realized we had the house to ourselves. The new plan was to divide and conquer, and we laughed as we ran up the lawn toward the giant house. Inside, a winding staircase swooped upward and a balcony overlooked the marble foyer lit by a glittering chandelier. Tina led us down the hallway to the kitchen, where Alex flung open the refrigerator door. He grabbed two cans of beer and handed one to me.

"What the hell are you doing?" Tina asked. "My dad is going to know those are missing."

The beer in Alex's hand hissed as he popped it open.

"Oops. Too late." He grinned.

"You guys!" Tina whined, but she was too drunk to really care.

Soon Alex and Tina were upstairs in her room while Emily and I sat on the floor in Tina's brother's room. I stared at the giant aquarium in front of me.

"What's in the aquarium?"

"You don't want to know," Emily said, taking the beer out of my hand.

"Why?" I asked. A chill went through my body. "Is that a fucking snake?"

She took a chug on my beer then nodded. I hated snakes.

"What kind is it?"

"Some kind of python," she said with a shrug. "He feeds it mice. It's disgusting."

I forced myself to look away and spotted a row of crates filled with records along one wall. For a rich kid, Tina's brother had great taste in music. The record collection was killer—Alice Cooper, Bowie, The Faces. He even had Hendrix's

Band of Gypsys. I dug through crates, ignoring Emily, until she let out a dramatic sigh, pulled out *Eric Clapton* and handed it to me.

"Here. Put this on," she said, pushing the record toward me.

"No thanks."

"Why not?" she slurred.

"I'm not into white-boy boogie rock."

"Oh, you know what? Screw you."

"Oh, come on." I grinned. "You know it's soulless shit."

She was climbing into the bed and not really listening. I put on the Stones' *Between the Buttons* and passed her a beer. She giggled and rolled her eyes as she stretched out. I wondered what she was laughing at when "Let's Spend the Night Together" started and I realized how badly I had screwed up.

"Oh yeah. Sorry about that." I grinned again. "Try not to read too much into it."

"No problem." She giggled coolly, sipping her beer. I lay down next to her and by "Ruby Tuesday" we were making out. I slipped my hand up her shirt and kissed her neck but she was a dead fish. No response. She must have figured that rather than stop me and give me a chance to talk her into anything she'd just freeze me out. I knew how to get a response. I'd slide my hand down between her legs and wait for her to grab my wrist and stop me. I groped in the dark, searching for some boundaries. I'd been shut down. Alex definitely figured this one out and stuck me with the dead end again.

The record was over but Tina's hysterical moans shattered any awkward silence. The bed in the next room thundered as Tina groaned in no particular rhythm. It seemed to last forever. Emily fought back a smile as we kissed. I broke from her and pushed the hair out of my eyes.

"Goddamn. You might need to go check on your friend."

This made her laugh. I flipped the record over and realized

the booze had worn me out. I felt heavy and spaced out. Back in bed I decided to give up on her. We lay side by side listening to "Who's Been Sleeping Here" until she passed out.

When I was sure Emily was asleep I slipped out of bed, put my pants on and crept down the hallway. The door to Tina's bedroom dragged along thick carpeting as I pushed it open. Posters of the Stones and Led Zeppelin lined the walls and a glass bong sat on the dresser. In the bed, Alex lay on his side with his bare back to me, one arm flung across Tina. She snored loudly with black eyeliner smeared under her eyes. I poked Alex.

"Wake up, man."

He jerked awake and squinted at me in the dark.

"What?"

"Come on. Get up."

Alex watched Tina, careful not to wake her, as he worked himself out of the tangle of sheets. I handed him his pants and he stumbled into them as we snuck from the room. He stopped me in the hallway.

"Are we leaving?"

"Not yet," I said. "But look at this place. She's loaded. Let's check it out."

"Are you fucking serious?" he asked. "These chicks are pretty cool. You want to rob them?"

"It's no big deal. We take a few pieces of jewelry. Her mother won't miss it."

Alex rubbed his eyes.

"Shit," he whispered. "You're right. Good thinking."

Down the hallway, we slipped into Tina's parents' bedroom and turned on a light by the bed. Alex dug through a wooden jewelry box and picked over the rings, holding a few to the light, before stuffing a couple into his pocket. I found a roll of cash in an old film canister in the top of the closet and grabbed a man's watch that I later gave to my father as a Christmas gift.

"Damn, man," Alex whispered. "They're going to know it was us."

"So what?" I fired back. "Then they'll have to tell Tina's parents that they had us over and they aren't going to do that. So even if they figure it out they can't do anything about it."

Alex jerked open a dresser drawer and knocked over a few framed pictures of Tina and her family. I pulled my head out of the closet and put one finger to my lips.

After we picked over everything, we padded down the hallway. Emily lay curled up in a ball facing the wall in Tina's brother's bed. I stripped down to my boxers and slipped into bed next to her.

In the morning I woke up alone. Alex talked loudly down in the kitchen and the girls laughed at anything he said. I dressed, then trudged down the carpeted stairs and sat at the table. The girls made breakfast and I didn't say much as everyone ate. I wasn't hungover yet but it was on the way. When we finished, Emily cleaned up while Tina brought down their luggage. I heard her scream from upstairs.

"Holy shit!"

I was sure that Tina had figured out what Alex and I had stolen during the night. My hangover hit full force and I felt sweaty and nauseous. I eyed my car sitting outside in the street. Emily stopped scrubbing a plate and yelled up the stairs to Tina.

"What's wrong?"

Tina stumbled down the stairs with a giant suitcase and stuck her head into the kitchen. Her eyes were huge with panic.

"It's almost eleven," she gasped. "My grandpa is going to be here any minute."

This sent the girls scrambling to clean up, cram things into the luggage, unplug the coffeepot, clean out the refrigerator and double-check that all the doors and windows were locked. Alex and I sat at the table. I lay my head down, forehead in my hand. Alex drank a cup of coffee and sat cocked back in the chair with his shoes on the edge of the table. He pulled a cigarette from a pack, lit the end with a silver lighter from a bowl on the counter, pocketed the lighter and exhaled a cloud of smoke.

"Alex, can you put this key in the mailbox?" Tina asked. She tossed a silver key to him.

"You know that isn't safe," he said. The tone was preachy and concerned without a trace of threat. "Someone could find it and clean the place out."

"It's for Nancy next door. She's going to feed my brother's snake."

"Will do," Alex said with a wink.

Emily and I said good-bye. I promised to call her. Tina and Alex made out like lovers on a sinking ship. Me and Alex passed Grandpa as we pulled out of the cul-de-sac. He glared at us with a look that said he knew exactly where we were coming from even though he arrived too late to prove it. I stared at him from behind my dark black sunglasses. *Sorry, you old fucker.*

Alex unloaded two fistfuls of gold jewelry from the pockets of his jeans and dumped them in his lap.

"We're never going back there again." Alex laughed as we rounded the corner.

"Yeah, we are," I told him. "They left a key in the mailbox."

Now I sat at the kitchen table at Keith's and stared at a cockroach as it climbed across a dirty pan and into an empty

Hormel chili can. Keith's mom, Suzy, leaned against the counter, clutching her pink bathrobe closed with one hand. She was in her forties and still looked pretty good, tiny and tan with bleached-out hair. She never seemed to change out of her pink bathrobe except to go to work at the dry cleaners.

Keith came downstairs, freshly showered. He stood in the middle of the kitchen and tied a folded-up bandanna around his head to hold down his long, soaking wet hair.

"You look like an idiot," Suzy said.

"Shut up," Keith said, straightening the headband. "I think it looks cool."

Suzy rolled her eyes and pulled a drag off a long cigarette. "Christ. You look more like your father every day."

We couldn't argue. None of us had ever seen Keith's father. Keith's mom had always been single. His entire life Keith had put up with a string of Suzy's shitty boyfriends. They ranged from an accountant who Keith hated to a stock car racer who Keith loved.

"Go back upstairs," Keith told her. He glared at her from the corner of his eye.

She rolled her eyes again and grunted while exhaling a cloud of smoke. The two noises together sounded like a car stalling in her chest. Keith set a paper bag with a bottle in it on the table in front of me and Frenchy.

"I got Alex a welcome home gift."

"Crown Royal?" Frenchy asked.

"Yes, sir." Keith grinned.

"And where did you get the money for that?" Suzy snarled at Keith.

"I work, Mom."

"And Alex," she grumbled out of the side of her mouth, lips clenched on the cigarette. "Breaking into people's houses. He ought to be ashamed of himself."

Keith raised his head to roll his own eyes then looked back down at the kitchen table.

"You better not being doing shit like that, Keith. You're nineteen years old. You're on your own now, mister. You're not my fucking problem anymore."

She leaned against the kitchen counter and sipped her coffee. Keith traced a line of spilled sugar on the table with his finger.

"You go to jail and I ain't bailing you out. I don't have the money," she said. "I may have to start fucking your friends to pay the rent."

Frenchy sat up.

"Suzy. I got paid today."

"Oh, fuck off, Pete," she hissed. "You wouldn't know what to do with it if I gave it to you."

She pulled her robe closed at the top then crossed her arms over her chest.

"Seriously," Frenchy said. He stood up and reached for his wallet.

"How much do you make over there?" Suzy asked.

"Ma!" Keith barked. "Just get the fuck out of here! Isn't *Sonny and Cher* starting?"

Suzy's head spun toward the clock.

"Oh my God!" she shrieked.

She leaned over Keith, stubbed her cigarette out in the ashtray then ran barefoot across the kitchen and up the stairs.

Keith swept his hand across the table, wiping the sugar to the floor. It was quiet for a long time except for the sound of a TV upstairs. Keith stole two packs of Suzy's cigarettes from a kitchen cabinet then said, "Let's head over to Alex's. He should be home now." I said yeah and Frenchy shrugged, and we all piled out the door and into my car.

FOUR

sprung

alex arrived HOME FROM PRISON WITH TWO SHOE BOXES. ONE WAS FILLED WITH PICTURES OF HIS NEW SON, THE OTHER WITH PICTURES OF ALL THE WOMEN HE MET WHILE LOCKED UP. I STOOD AGAINST A WALL AT HIS WELCOME-HOME PARTY, TOOK A LONG PULL OFF A WARM CAN OF BEER AND WONDERED OUT LOUD TO FRENCHY HOW A GUY SERVING EIGHT MONTHS FOR BREAKING AND ENTERING MET MORE WOMEN THAN I DID OUT ON THE STREET.

"It's pretty amazing, isn't it?" Frenchy agreed.

He thought about something then spoke up.

"What are you gonna say to him?"

"I don't know," I said.

"This is a bad idea. I really shouldn't have brought you."

Across the room Alex ran both hands over his slicked-back hair. He flipped a menthol cigarette into his mouth and I caught a glimpse of a cross tattoo on his forearm. That was new. The tattoo made him look like an ex-con or some tough guy from the other side of town, which I suppose he always was, really.

We were all born in Forest Park but in the sixties our parents moved us across town to Locust Point. Alex's family never left. His old man was a drunk and a gambler and loved that he lived near Pimlico racecourse. He didn't care that his son was one of the only white kids left at Forest Park High School. By the time Alex dropped out, he was trying to fit in by acting black. I guess he never stopped. To us, he really was black. He ironed his jeans, wore bright button-up shirts and doused himself with cologne. He kept his black hair shorter than the rest of us and slicked it back instead of wearing it long. He smoked menthol cigarettes and listened to R&B. He pretended not to like rock 'n' roll. Worst of all, he hated Black Sabbath.

I scanned the crowd in Alex's mother's tiny basement. All of Alex's relatives were crooks. Most of them were older guys with bad teeth and faded blue prison tattoos. They had all been in jail at some point but got out, married one of the busted-looking chicks hanging around and settled down, which to them meant cutting out violent crime and sticking to simple robbery.

A pair of boys ran past spraying each other with water guns until the smaller one stumbled and smacked his forehead into a table holding a cake that said "Welcome Home Alex." On the other side of the table a skinny guy in a denim vest and no shirt showed off a long-barrel revolver to a bald musclehead in a Kool cigarettes tank top.

Alex's mom looked older than the last time I saw her. Silver streaked her curly brown hair. She knotted her fingers together nervously as she talked with one of Alex's aunts. Alex's dad stood next to her. He sipped a can of Coors and grunted now and then. His glasses and thick beard covered his face and made it hard to tell just how much Alex looked like him. I couldn't remember if I'd ever heard him talk. Mostly he hid in the garage or lumbered around the house mumbling.

"It's the math of the whole thing I don't get," I said to Frenchy and Keith.

"Math of what thing?" Frenchy asked.

"How did Alex even come in contact with that many women? He was in jail."

"Why don't you ask him?" Keith said.

I was dying to ask Alex about it but couldn't bring myself to do it. Frenchy was right. After eight months in County I was probably the last person he wanted to see. In fact, I knew it.

"Well, well, well," a voice behind me slurred. "If it ain't the kiddie table."

Alex's uncle Danny slapped Keith on the back then crossed his arms and stared at me. His dark hair hung down to his shoulders. A chicken drumstick jutted from his crooked mouth, hidden behind a thick handlebar mustache.

"What are you doing back in town?" he asked me, his mouth full of chicken.

"Just came to see Alex."

"He know you're here?"

"Not yet."

Danny grunted and looked me over while he chewed. A piece of chicken snagged in his mustache then fell, landing on the front of his Corvette T-shirt. Looking at him now, it was hard to believe he was our idol when we were kids. Back then he was a football star. Scouts from the University of Maryland once came to Forest Park High to watch him play. On a field trip to Memorial Stadium, the Baltimore Colts' quarterback Johnny Unitas even said Danny had a great arm.

But by junior year of high school, Danny was smoking a sack of weed every day. He stopped going to school and showing up to practice. Then he got arrested for stealing a keg of beer out of the back of the Crown Pub and Coach Dunlop had to bail him out. A month later he dropped out of school and began breaking into houses and businesses with the rest of Alex's uncles. But Danny had the lowest IQ of any of Alex's uncles, which meant he also had the biggest rap sheet. He'd never gotten away with anything. Now he was twenty-seven years old, on parole and living with Alex's grandmother. Once and only once did I let Alex convince me to bring Danny with us on a job. We were at Alex's welcome-home-from-jail party as a result.

"Didn't you just get out of County too?" Keith asked Danny.

"Last week." He shrugged.

"Was this for breaking into the Old Towne Bar?" Keith asked him. Danny nodded.

"How'd you guys get caught?" I asked.

"Fucking daylight savings time or whatever the hell it is," he spit. He stopped to lick the chicken grease off his fingers. "We busted in the place and the motherfucker was still open. I'd have run but the owner had a shotgun on me. I'm still fast but I ain't that fast."

He tossed the chicken bone on the table then opened a can of beer. He took a long pull off the beer then wiped his mouth with the back of his hand.

"Well, Patrick. I know if I was Alex I sure wouldn't want your ass at my welcome-home party. Personally, I don't think he's gonna want to see you after the mess you got him into."

I spoke slowly, choking on each word.

"This mess was your fault, not mine."

Danny shrugged and sucked on his beer. Foam clung to his mustache.

"Well, it was your plan, bud. Not mine. This shit went sideways on your watch. Know what I mean?"

My fists clenched. Frenchy shot Keith a worried look. Across the crowd, Alex sat alone on the couch for the first time all night. This was my shot. I left Danny standing by the wall and wove my way through the crowd and across the room.

"I hear you got quite a collection of photos," I said with a grin as I sat down next to Alex.

He looked up at me. If he was surprised to see me he didn't show it.

"Yeah," he mumbled.

"How'd you do it?"

"My cell mate. Crazy Mexican dude from downstate. His girlfriend would come up to visit all the time. She didn't like making the drive alone so she'd bring a friend."

"Makes sense."

"But he didn't want some other chick hanging around while he talked to his girl so he asked me if I would sit with her friend. It beat sitting in my cell. Me and this girl hit it off all right, and she started coming up a lot and writing me letters."

I nodded then leaned forward to get a look at the shoe box full of nudie photos. Frenchy rushed over and squeezed in next to me on the couch. Alex kept talking.

"Word got around and other guys started asking me to sit with their girlfriends' friends. One dude asked me to sit with his sister. Next thing I know I'm getting all these letters and pictures. Shit. It was hell writing back to all of them but I had nothing else to do."

The box was loaded with photos, mostly Polaroids of Mexican girls in little white nightgowns or skirts and high heels. There were a couple of shots of an older chick in red thigh-highs and lingerie bent over or spread-eagle on a bed. A hot brunette sucked on her finger and flashed her tits in a series of black-and-white photo booth shots. In one frame she gave a beer bottle a blow job. Had the thing in her mouth to the middle of the label. Frenchy was flipping out.

"Damn," Frenchy groaned. "This is better than the old *Playboy*s under my bed."

"Those are *my* old *Playboy*s, asshole." Alex grinned. "I want those back."

He took a long drag on his cigarette.

"You know I'm a father now, right?" he asked, killing the mood just as I gave a close-up look to a blonde pushing her size-Ds together and smiling at the camera.

"Remember that blonde I was seeing? Vickie? She got pregnant before I went in."

I remembered Vickie. Tiny. Blonde. Personality like wallpaper.

"Yeah. She was cool," I lied. I quickly looked around the room. "Is she here?"

"Nah." He shrugged. "She and the baby moved back to Florida to be near her family."

Alex grabbed the box of photos off my lap and replaced it with a half-empty box with TOMMY scrawled across the top in black marker.

The top photo was a black-and-white hospital shot. The screaming prune-wrinkled face looked like Alex, I guess. It had his tan skin and wisps of black hair. I flipped through a parade of shots of people holding the baby. I turned them slowly and pretended to be interested.

The kid grew older as I looked through the pictures. I flipped to a photo of him sitting in a high chair and nearly choked. His olive skin was much darker and his frizzy black hair stuck straight up. He looked like Sly fucking Stone or Jimi Hendrix on the cover of *Axis.*

Lil' Tommy was black.

I didn't know whether to tell Alex the kid wasn't his or just keep my mouth shut. Maybe while he was locked up he convinced himself that this was his son and had fallen in love with him. What if I told him and he lost his mind and had a breakdown or something? I decided to keep my mouth shut.

"He's really something," I stammered.

"Yeah? Think he looks like me?"

"Oh yeah. Sure," I lied again. "Totally."

Alex snatched the box of photos from my lap.

"Same ol' Patrick," he said, shaking his head. "Still a bull-shitter."

"What do you mean?"

Alex leaned forward. He pushed a photo into my face.

"Look at him, man. This kid looks like Joe Frazier. There's no way he's mine."

"Okay." I grinned. "Caught me on that one."

Alex lit another cigarette.

"What the hell are you doing here, anyway?"

"I just came to see you."

"Bullshit. You didn't drive all the way down from New York City just to see me."

"All right," I said, leaning back. "I have an idea."

"Is this the one where we rob my girlfriend's house while her family is on vacation? If so, I can tell you how it ends up. Sixteen stitches from a python bite and eight months in the joint. Well, not for you, of course."

I had that coming.

"It was just as much Danny's fault as it was mine."

Alex shrugged.

"Honestly, man," he said. "I just got out four hours ago for some shit you got me into and then you show up trying to drag me into some new bullshit plan. What the fuck are you trying to do?"

"I'm trying to help you out. You know, make it up to you."

Alex glared at me out of the corner of his eye as he dragged on his cigarette. Then he looked over at Keith and Frenchy.

"What about those guys?" Alex asked.

"We're gonna need them too."

He sipped his beer.

"This idea is that big?"

"No. It's that good."

"Well. Let's hear it."

"I want to rob Led Zeppelin."

Alex leaned forward and stubbed out his cigarette on the top of an empty can. Then he slumped back into the sofa, looked me in the eye and pointed toward the door.

"Get the fuck out of here."

FIVE

soul training

"the doors WERE NEVER ON *SOUL TRAIN*," KEITH SHOUTED AS I SLIPPED INTO ALEX'S BEDROOM. I PULLED THE DOOR CLOSED BEHIND ME.

"They were on the same episode as Ike and Tina Turner," Alex said. "I saw it when I was in County."

They were stoned and standing in the middle of the room arguing. Al Green played on a turntable sitting on a table under a poster of Curtis Mayfield. Alex's room was always a mess, except for his clothes, which were pressed and hung up in the closet. A clear plastic bag on the floor read BALTIMORE COUNTY JAIL: PERSONAL BELONGINGS. Inside were the clothes Alex had on the night the cops nabbed him.

"They played 'Light My Fire,'" Alex teased Keith. He turned his head and winked at Frenchy. Keith rubbed his forehead. He looked distraught.

"Were the Doors ever on *Soul Train*, Patrick?" Keith asked me. "They weren't on there, were they? 'Cause I hate that fucking show."

His bleary eyes pleaded for me to tell him it wasn't true. It wasn't.

"No. They weren't."

"Aww, come on," Frenchy groaned. "Why'd you have to tell him?"

"He looked like he was gonna cry."

"Come on, Keith," Alex said. "You ever see white people on that show?"

Alex loved winding Keith up and poor dumb Keith always fell for it. It could be anything. He only got mad the time we made him believe *Hawaii Five-O* was canceled. He didn't speak to any of us for a week.

It took some time but I had managed to convince Alex to at least hear my plan. A few factors worked in my favor. Having just been walked out of the gates at Baltimore County Jail hours earlier Alex was taking a hard look at his future. It looked like shit. He was a high school dropout and now an ex-con. He was facing miles of floors to mop or, if he was lucky, a backbreaking job unloading freighters down at the Inner Harbor. And even if he did come up with a decent scam that didn't involve me, he'd be stuck working with his uncle Danny. The few months Alex had just spent locked up with that dumbass probably convinced him that wasn't going to work.

"These guys know about your idea?" Alex asked, jerking a thumb toward Frenchy and Keith.

"Nope," Keith said. "What idea?"

I took a look around the room.

"I've been working for Mancini's brother Carmine in New York City. He owns a catering business. We set up all the food backstage at concerts and political events and shit. A few months ago I worked a Zeppelin concert."

"You got to see Zeppelin?" Keith asked.

"Pay attention, man. So after the show, me and another guy are taking down the tables when I hear an argument going on down the hall. I peek around the corner and there's Lenny, the guy who books the shows. He's standing there arguing with this huge, bald British guy. I didn't know if Lenny was being robbed or what. Lenny hands the British guy this briefcase and the guy opens it. It's filled to the top with cash. Then the guy stomps off towards the dressing rooms.

"I walk over and ask Lenny if everything is cool. He's a little shaken up. Standing against the wall smoking. He tells me that was Zeppelin's manager making sure they got paid what they were promised. Says their manager always yells like that. Then I ask him about the cash. He tells me that Zeppelin always get paid in cash. Always. That night, it was over one hundred thousand dollars."

"Goddamn," Keith said, shaking his head.

"So what are you saying?" Frenchy asked.

"We rob Led Zeppelin."

No one said anything. Finally, Keith laughed.

"You motherfuckers. First you make me think Jim Morrison was on *Soul Train* and now this bullshit. Nice try, guys."

"I'm serious."

"How are you guys going to rob Zeppelin?" Frenchy asked. "What are you going to do? Fly to England?"

"Don't need to. They're playing Baltimore on Monday."

Alex hadn't said a word.

"But I thought rock bands usually got paid by check or something?" Frenchy asked.

"Not Zeppelin. Their manager makes sure they always get paid cash."

"So how much are we talking?" Alex asked.

"From the sound of it, maybe one hundred thousand, split four ways."

"Goddamn!" Keith yelled. "Twenty-five thousand dollars each? Shit. I'm in."

"You didn't want to rob a bank but now you wanna do this?" Alex said, crossing his arms.

"Whoa! Whoa!" Frenchy stood up. "What the fuck! You guys were gonna rob a bank? What the hell is wrong with you?"

"It was just an idea a long time ago," I said. "Calm down."

"How are you gonna pull this off?" Alex asked.

"The show starts at eight and probably goes until midnight. They probably get out of there even later. The way I see it, every bank in town is closed by then. That means their manager has to hold on to all that money until the next day."

Heads nodded around the room.

"That gives us roughly eight or nine hours to get to that cash before it goes in the bank."

"But where will the money be?" Alex asked. "You don't know who has it, where they take it, what they look like. Hell, you don't even know where they're staying."

"Right," I agreed. "First, we need to find out who collects the money after the show and what they carry it in. I saw it in a briefcase but maybe it changes. Then, we need to find out which hotel they're staying in and see if the person with the money keeps it in his room or sticks it in a safe deposit. That's where we'll get it."

"Sounds easy enough," Keith said.

"Sounds easy?" Alex said. "Stealing a safe deposit box from a hotel is a lot different than tearing a car stereo out of a Nova, Keith."

"That's not even the hard part," I explained. "Zeppelin travels with hard-core security. These guys are brutal. British goons who will kick your fucking head in. They answer to Zeppelin's manager, Peter Grant. He's over six feet tall. Three hundred pounds. He's an ex-bouncer and an ex-wrestler. If we get caught fucking him around, we're finished."

"Forget it," Frenchy erupted. "This is insane. Zeppelin are the biggest band on the planet right now. The biggest! How are you gonna pull this off? There's no way in hell."

"When have you ever heard of a rock band being robbed?" I asked. "Name one."

"That's because it's impossible!" Frenchy argued.

"No. It's because no one else ever thought of it," I replied. "They won't see it coming."

"So what the hell, man?" Keith groaned. "How are we gonna pull this off?"

Alex crossed his arms and watched me as I talked.

"We plant one team backstage to see how Zeppelin gets paid, who carries the cash, what happens to it," I explained. "The other team waits at the hotel to grab the money."

"What are the teams?" Alex asked.

"The way I see it, me and Frenchy will be the backstage team. Alex and Keith will be the hotel team."

Alex lit a smoke and laughed out loud.

"No fucking way, man. I'm out."

"Why?" I said. "You got a better idea?"

"I already took the fall for you once. It ain't happening again. You want me in? You go on the hotel team."

"Alex, you're the only one who could get in that hotel room and you're definitely the only one who could get to a safe deposit box."

"No fucking chance," Alex said, belching out a thick cloud of smoke.

"Would you feel better if I worked with you on the hotel team?" I asked.

Alex nodded.

"So you're going to send Keith backstage with Led Zepplin?" I asked. Alex knew that was a horrible idea.

"I like that idea." Keith grinned.

"No way," Alex said. He looked at me. "You'll just have to do both."

"Fine. I'll scout the backstage with Frenchy then work with you guys to get the cash."

The record on the turntable ended and the needle hissed as the record spun beneath it. Outside the bedroom door Alex's welcome-home party carried on without him. Keith spoke up first.

"Where do we start?"

Frenchy jumped in. "I think we need to figure out how to get backstage first."

"I have a plan for that," I told them.

"And we need to check out the hotel," Alex said. "Do you know which hotel they're using?"

"I don't know but I know someone who will," I answered. I pulled the bright yellow Misty Mountain Hoppers Led Zeppelin Fan Club flier out of the pocket where I'd left it since tearing it down at Record Barn. Frenchy shook his head.

"No, no. That's a horrible idea," he said.

"Yeah, man." Alex laughed. "She's gonna want to see you even less than I did."

They were both right.

SIX

jimi the bear

the waiters AT THE SEAFOOD RESTAURANT STARED AT MY TORN-UP JEANS AND BLACK SABBATH T-SHIRT THE NEXT DAY AS THE HOSTESS LED ME TO A CORNER BOOTH. I WASN'T BOTHERED. I WAS STILL THINKING ABOUT ALEX'S PARTY THE NIGHT BEFORE. I DIDN'T CARE WHAT ANYONE SAID. DANNY WAS MORE TO BLAME THAN THAT DAMN SNAKE FOR WHAT WENT DOWN THE NIGHT WE ROBBED TINA'S HOUSE.

We did it on New Year's Eve. Tina and her family would be back on New Year's Day so that was our last chance to do it. I'd gone out with Emily every night that week and was meeting her at a New Year's Eve party later that night. I promised I would be there before midnight.

I only agreed to let Danny come with us because he drove a pickup truck and we wanted to be able to haul everything. It was late and most of the houses were dark. We could see the front door to Tina's house in the distance. The three of us were sitting sandwiched together in the front seat of his truck watching the street when I realized what a dumb idea it was to bring him.

"I don't see why the fuck Santa would use elves," Danny said.

Alex giggled and crushed buds into a pipe with the corner of a candy cane–striped lighter.

"Seriously," Danny kept on. "How the fuck are elves supposed to make toys with those chubby little fingers?"

I stared through the frosted windshield at a light-up reindeer staked in the front yard of a huge house.

"Dwarves have chubby fingers." I sighed. "Elves don't."

"Wrong, Patrick," Danny spat, his frosted breath blowing in my face. "I did dishes at Denny's with that little elf motherfucker and he has fat fingers."

"That's because he's a dwarf, dumbass."

Danny stared at the floor and thought for a second.

"If he's a dwarf, then what the hell is an elf?"

Once Alex was good and stoned, he climbed out of the truck and crunched off down the icy street toward Tina's house. He dug the key out of the mailbox and then opened the door and slipped inside. A minute later the garage door opened and Danny pulled the truck slowly up the street and into the garage. Alex closed the door behind us.

We kept the lights off in the house as me and Alex loaded up the truck. Danny walked around knocking paintings off the wall, searching for a safe. I was disconnecting the stereo in Tina's brother's room when Alex spotted the snake aquarium and panicked.

"We can't let Danny see this," he said. "Come on. We have to go."

"Why?" I asked, picking up the turntable.

"Because he's totally nuts over snakes. You didn't know

that?" Alex said. He grabbed the stereo and whipped the cable out of the wall.

"We have to get out of here. If he sees this thing—"

"Sees what thing?" Danny asked. He stood in the doorway holding a mounted moose head.

Alex stepped to the left to block Danny's view but it was too late. The moose head thumped to the ground and Danny charged over to the aquarium. He flipped open the heavy lip, shoved his arm inside and lifted the cover to a small habitat. A coiled giant white snake hissed from the corner. Alex and I backed toward the door. Danny grabbed the snake behind the head and all twelve feet of it uncoiled as he lifted it out of the cage.

"Hot shit!" he said. "This is an albino carpet python. We can get a ton for this thing."

"We're not stealing a snake, man," I said, keeping my distance.

"Are you nuts? There are probably rare snake dealers in Arizona who will pay thousands for this guy."

He stared into the snake's eyes. There was no way we were taking the snake.

"And where are you going to keep it until then?" I argued. "How are you going to ship it? You don't know anything about this shit so just put it back."

Danny ranted about Australian pythons, reptile breeding and international shipping procedures for live animals, most of which he probably made up. When me and Alex refused to help him carry the heated aquarium, Danny dropped the snake on the bed and stomped down the stairs. The house shook as the garage door raised and Danny sped out of the garage. Tires squealed down the driveway and the truck fishtailed when it hit the icy street. Danny lost control and the truck careened off a parked car. He oversteered and spun out in the neighbor's front yard, mowing over the light-up reindeer. He got the truck back on the street and sped away.

Alex and I were grabbing whatever we could carry when the front door opened. Flashlights circled the room and two cops yelled for us to stop. I bolted to the right and ran down the long hallway through the kitchen, then out the back door and across the dark yard. Alex was cornered. He turned and ran back up the stairs. The cops tackled him, knocking him across Tina's brother's bed and on top of the twelve-foot albino python. I was climbing the backyard fence when the snake sunk its teeth into Alex's arm. I swear I heard him scream.

I shook off the memory just as the waitress grunted a hello and set down a glass of water, slopping most of it on the table. She never looked at me. Her dark ponytail swung as she turned her head toward the front door and a family who looked fresh from church entered.

"I'm ready to order," I told her.

She mumbled something and rifled through the front of her red apron, pulling out a pen and a notepad. After flipping a few pages she looked up, stared at me for a few seconds then spoke.

"What the fuck do *you* want?"

I sort of expected that.

"How have you been, Emily?"

Her elbow jutted out as she slapped her hand on her hip. She rolled her blues.

"What can I get you?"

"I'm back in town for a bit and thought I would come by."

"Great. When are you leaving?"

"Not sure. I came in for Alex's welcome-home party. Didn't see you there."

"Is that supposed to be funny?"

"Yeah," I said, looking down. "Sorry. It was a bad joke."

She stared at me. Her glossed lips popped on her chewing gum.

"Listen," I said. "I'm really sorry about how everything went down."

"Which part? The part when you and Alex robbed my best friend's house or the part when you stood me up on New Year's Eve and left town without ever talking to me again?"

"I had nothing to do with what happened at Tina's," I lied. "And I had to leave town. I had a great job lined up in New York that couldn't wait. I tried getting in touch with you. You never returned any of my calls."

"I was mad."

"Let me make it up to you," I said.

Emily's boss yelled to her from behind the counter.

"I got to go," she said, turning to walk away.

"Wait. What are you doing tonight?"

"It's Sunday. You know what I'm doing. I'm going to my sister's."

"Is she still running that Led Zeppelin fan club?"

"Yes. And you know it's called the Misty Mountain Hoppers."

"Can I come with you?"

She stopped and looked up at me.

"Why? You don't like Zeppelin."

"Would coming to the meeting be punishment enough for you to forgive me?"

"Maybe," she said.

"Then maybe I'll do it," I said.

When she walked away, I yanked the yellow flier from the Record Barn out of my pocket, crumpled it and tossed it under the booth.

* * *

Emily's sister Anna lived in a boxy apartment above a car parts store on a busy street. Concrete steps shot straight up the back to a long, tiled hallway. The apartment was in rough shape but Anna had done her best to dress it up. Bright paint covered each room. Yellow in the living room. Red in the kitchen. Green in the bedroom. Tapestries and black-light posters covered the walls along with photos of Led Zeppelin. A half-finished mural on the living room wall showed Jimi Hendrix in the sky above portraits of Led Zeppelin. Anna was a terrible painter and Jimi looked more like Yogi Bear.

Anna was short and dumpy, and even though she was only in her twenties she looked older. She shuffled past in a flowing yellow skirt that reached her ankles just above bare feet covered in weird jewelry. Trinkets and braids dangled in her ratty brown hair. Emily was wild and energetic but Anna was dull and almost always incredibly stoned. She held a dopey grin on her face, especially as she cut me off and talked over me. She did that to everyone. Most of her sentences trailed off as she fumbled to pin some hokey spiritual bullshit to everything.

She led us through the beaded curtains dangling in the doorway and into the living room.

"I hear you are living in New York City, Patrick. How is it?"

"It's good."

"Ugh. I don't like that place. It's such a negative energy trap."

Emily covered her mouth to stifle a laugh. I didn't know what to say.

"What's your sign anyway?" Anna asked.

Virgo. But I hated astrology.

"I don't know."

"You don't know your sign?"

I looked at Yogi Hendrix on the wall.

"I think I'm the Bear."

"The Bear? Is that from the Chinese zodiac?"

There was a knock at the door.

"Sorry, guys! That must be Kyle," Anna said. "Help yourself to a beer or a hash brownie. We'll fire up Babe later."

"What's Babe?" I asked Emily when Anna was gone.

Emily pointed to a giant blue bong nearly four feet tall in the corner.

"She nicknamed it Babe the Blue Ox."

"Your sister is insane."

"You're the one who wanted to come with me." She grinned.

The rest of the Misty Mountain Hoppers slowly showed up. They were a sad pack of hippies. Guys who got the "burn out" part down but forgot the "fade away."

There was Carl, a scrawny guy with one arm in a sling, dirty glasses that covered his entire face and a cheap cowboy hat who whined about the food while Manuel, a three-hundred-pound Mexican kid, bitched about the hot weather. Steve and Stacy, a brother-and-sister duo, talked about wheatgrass juice. Jim paced around the apartment in tight, black bell-bottoms. He looked like an ex-con or at least a psycho. He wore a pentagram ring on a tattooed hand and carried an Aleister Crowley book. The other stragglers looked like they just woke up at the bus station and didn't have anywhere else to go. Everyone smoked pot.

Kyle was the leader. He looked bookish, with long brown hair, Lennon-style glasses and a few turquoise rings. He sat cross-legged in a corner chair in his white pants, an ugly paisley shirt and an expensive-looking tan suede vest. Anna brought him a cup of tea and he nodded but never looked up from his stack of notes.

"Okay, everyone," Kyle said. He stood in the middle of the

living room. We all sat like kindergarteners on the floor around him.

"Tomorrow night is Zeppelin at the Civic Center. I'll be driving a load of people down in my van and Carl can take a few people in his truck."

Kyle reminded everyone to meet at Anna's the next day so they could drive down together and then asked Steve and Stacy for a report on the sign they were supposed to make that said MISTY MOUNTAIN HOPPERS LOVE LED ZEPPELIN. Kyle looked disgusted when neither one of them remembered and that led to a discussion on the strength of last week's wine, which took a bizarre right turn into a talk about Carl's habit of pissing his pants when he got really stoned.

"Now has anyone had any luck figuring out where the band is staying in New York City the rest of the week?" Kyle asked. "We were all supposed to make some calls this week."

Everyone stared at the ground like kids who had forgotten to do their homework.

"They are playing Friday, Saturday and Sunday at Madison Square Garden, guys. We are driving up for Saturday's show and it would be nice to know where the band is staying so we can stake out the lobby. Anyone have any ideas?"

"How hard could it be to figure that out?" I whispered to Emily.

"You think you know?" she said, grabbing my hand.

"Well, I'm sure I could find out if I really gave a shit."

She turned to Kyle.

"Kyle. Patrick says he can find out where Zeppelin is staying."

"Oh yeah?" Kyle said, looking down his glasses at me. "And how are you going to do that?"

I hadn't really thought about it. I figured that Carmine

could find out. He'd been catering concerts for years in New York City.

"I know a caterer," I said.

Kyle pushed his glasses back up his nose and shook his head.

"I don't see how that's going to work."

"Gimme the phone."

I dialed Carmine's office but he didn't answer. I tried the main office and Louise picked up. She put me on hold for a few minutes then popped back on to give me the address. I knew what she was going to say before she said it. I hung up and walked back into the living room.

"Drake Hotel. Park Avenue and Fifty-sixth."

Everyone looked surprised. A few of them doubted me but didn't have any better answers. Emily grabbed my hand again when I sat back down.

"Why do you come to these things?" I asked her later after the meeting had ended. We were standing in the kitchen grabbing beers from the fridge.

"Mostly because I like hanging out with my sister. Besides, it's not so bad. Free beer and pot. Beats being at home."

She leaned against the kitchen counter.

"How did Kyle become the leader of this group?" I asked.

"He's the only one who's met Jimmy Page. He sold Jimmy Page a guitar last year."

"No shit?"

"Ask him about it. Believe me, he loves telling the story."

"No thanks. I don't want to encourage him."

Emily looked around the party.

"Hey, Kyle," she yelled into the living room. "Patrick wants to hear about the time you met Jimmy."

I glared at her as I walked toward the living room. Kyle sat cross-legged on the floor taking a drag from Babe the blue bong. He turned around when he finished.

"Have *you* met Jimmy?" he asked me.

"Nope."

"You really should, man. He's amazing. I met him last year."

"Is that when you sold him a guitar?"

"Yeah. My dad had given me a sixty-four Stratocaster when I was in college. I never learned to play it. I'd actually forgotten about it. When I got back from Europe I found it in a closet. A buddy told me it might be worth some money. I knew that Jimmy bought a lot of guitars on the road. I figured it might get me in to meet him. I mean, I just loved the idea that Jimmy would be playing a guitar that belonged to me."

"Totally," Anna said, nodding. "It would be like your energies were entwined."

I rolled my eyes.

"When Zeppelin came to town I brought the guitar to their hotel and waited in the lobby. I sat there all day until Richard Cole showed up."

"Who's Richard Cole?"

"You don't know who Richard Cole is?" Kyle scoffed.

I shook my head.

"He's Zeppelin's tour manager. He's a legend, man. So I showed him the guitar and he said he thought Jimmy might wanna buy it. He went upstairs to talk to Jimmy. I just hung out in the lobby. I waited a long time. I thought they forgot about me. Then Richard came back and told me to come upstairs. I figured we were going to his room but when the door opened Jimmy was sitting in a chair playing guitar through a teeny little amp. I was totally freaking out."

"Oh man," Carl said, shoving a hash brownie in his mouth.

"He was so small. I was surprised. He was maybe this tall," Kyle said, holding out his arm.

"He loved the guitar. Just loved it, man. He plugged it in and played some stuff on it for me. 'Dazed and Confused.' 'Thank You.' And a little song that hadn't even come out yet. Know what it was?"

I shrugged.

"Stairway to Heaven."

Everyone around us gasped, even though they'd heard it all before. Carl whistled loudly through a mouthful of hash brownies.

"Yep. I was the first person outside of Led Zeppelin and their crew to ever hear it."

Kyle looked pleased as shit, though he really had no actual way of knowing this.

"So he bought the guitar?" I asked.

Kyle looked annoyed.

"Yeah, he did, man. Three hundred dollars. Cash. Took it out of a briefcase filled with money. I've never seen so much money in my life. Must have been fifty thousand dollars."

"They really carry around that much cash?"

"It's Zeppelin, man," said Manuel, leaning in. He wheezed loudly while chewing on a potato chip. "They spend that shit on cars and guitars and the best freakin' drugs. They're rich, man."

"So where does the band stay when they're in Baltimore?" I asked.

"Where they always stay. The Hilton."

"They rent a whole floor or something?"

He gave me a suspicious look.

"Yeah. They take the top floor. Everyone stays there—the band, the crew, managers, everyone."

"Thanks for the story, Kyle," I said, walking away.

Me and Emily left a short time later just as the hash brownies laid waste to the Misty Mountain Hoppers. Anna passed out in a bean bag chair with her shirt off, and Manuel ate everything on the kitchen table including a can of whipped cream. Carl pissed his pants.

We laughed about the party on the drive to Emily's house. I felt fucking great. I missed hanging out with her. Hell, I missed Alex and Frenchy and Keith too. That cocky feeling crept back into my brain. The one that ran through me years ago when me and Alex were really working. That feeling like the world was one big scam and all you had to do was connect the dots, think fast and make the right moves as you pinballed around, and the whole thing wasn't nearly as hard as it looked because all of the other players were winging it just like you.

I couldn't stop myself from smiling as me and Emily made out in her driveway.

She pulled away.

"What are you grinning about?"

I couldn't tell her that I was going to rob the biggest rock 'n' roll band in the world so I just smiled and kissed her again.

crash landing

"**forget it,** FRENCHY," I YELLED, NOT LOOKING BACK AS I HURRIED UP THE CONCRETE CORRIDOR. "YOU'RE NOT BRITISH."

"Yes, I am, mate," he argued.

The accent sounded convincing. Still, there was no way I was going to let him fake being British. Backstage passes he had scored for us through a contest with WKTK and the Record Barn dangled around our necks. Frenchy adjusted his fake mustache and knocked a pair of aviator sunglasses off his face as he tried to keep up with me.

"Hang on a second," he said, stopping under the fluorescent lights in the hallway to pick up the sunglasses. He straightened up and smoothed the denim vest he wore over a button-up shirt. I stood in front of him.

"You can't be British," I lectured. "Are you listening to me? Led Zeppelin are British. Their managers and their crew are British. What if one of them asks you where you're from or where you went to school? You don't know shit about England."

The lights dimmed at the end of the tunnel and the crowd cheered. The sound of Zeppelin taking the stage poured down the corridor toward us in a tidal wave of noise.

"Listen," I said. "Stick to the story. Your name is Reginald Chamberlain. You're a rare-guitar dealer from Baltimore. You want to sell Jimmy Page your nineteen sixty Fender Telecaster. That's it."

"What if he doesn't want it?"

"Who gives a shit? We don't care if he buys it or not. We just need to hang around and watch them. See who has the money and find out where they're staying. Hopefully, we can ride with them back to the hotel."

He looked up at me.

"How does my mustache look?"

He lifted the guitar case and started up the corridor. Anyone backstage had already gathered at the side of the stage to watch Zeppelin, and me and Frenchy strode up the wide, empty hallway. Zeppelin charged through "Rock and Roll" and into "Celebration Day." The drums thundered off the concrete walls of the empty hallway as we marched toward the stage.

"What about the South?" Frenchy said. I could barely hear him over the music.

"What about it?"

"Can I be from the South? You know, use a Southern accent?"

"Let it go, Frenchy."

Roadies, bouncers and groupies crowded the side of the

stage. We slipped through and looked out into the Civic Center. Light washed over the faces of tens of thousands of screaming fans. Bodies filled every space from the floor to the ceiling and around the walls.

Jimmy Page stood facing the amps, his back to the crowd. Sweaty ringlets of dark hair surrounded his face. He wore black flares covered in embroidery and a small matching jacket with no shirt underneath. White symbols lined up the pant leg and around the cuffs of the jacket. His guitar hung low to his knees and he hunched over the neck, squeezing out the chords to "Celebration Day."

Frenchy turned to me and shouted over the music, "What about Brooklyn?"

"What?" I asked, cupping my ear.

"I've been working on a Brooklyn accent. This would be a great way to test it out. Can I use that?"

"Seriously, man. Stop it."

Zeppelin powered through "Black Dog" and "Over the Hills and Far Away" then launched into "Misty Mountain Hop." Robert Plant danced at the edge of the stage, wearing tight blue jeans and a tiny, matching vest. He twirled the microphone by the chord and pumped his hips at the crowd. They went wild.

The lights dimmed over the audience and Zeppelin eased into "Since I've Been Loving You." John Paul Jones's lazy bass lines rumbled across the stage. I tapped my foot and checked my watch. How long could they play?

The thought was broken up as a thick hand grabbed the back of my arm. A lanky guy in a white satin jacket poked his bearded face at me. His T-shirt read, "Edgewater Inn, Puget Sound."

"Who the fuck are you?" he asked, in a snarling British accent. "Where did you get this pass?"

He grabbed the pass around my neck and yanked me toward him until we were face-to-face.

"From WKTK," I stammered.

"What the fuck is that?" he asked, inspecting the back of my pass.

"It's a radio station here in Baltimore."

He locked eyes with me.

"Is it any good?"

"No. It's fucking awful."

"They play Zeppelin?"

"All the time," I answered, grinning.

He grunted and let go of my pass.

"Just stay the fuck out of the way," he barked as he stormed off. He turned and yelled back, "And tell your fucking friend."

A pair of groupies in short skirts and knee-high boots chased after him. Their voices trailed off.

"Richard! Hey, Richard! Wait!"

The opening chords of "The Song Remains the Same" erupted from the stage. Frenchy leaned over to talk to me.

"Who the fuck was that guy?"

"Richard Cole. Zeppelin's tour manager."

"He didn't look happy."

"No. He had a message for you."

"For me? What did he say?"

"Stay the fuck out of the way."

"Got it." Frenchy nodded.

Zeppelin closed the show with a blistering version of "Communication Breakdown" then charged offstage with the feedback from the instruments still pulsating through the arena. The backstage crowd swirled around us as the band rushed for the dressing room. The door slammed and those of us left in the hallway slumped against the walls.

Me and Frenchy waited with the crowd in the hallway. Now

and then a roadie or manager would go in or leave the room and the groupies would shriek "Jimmy" or "Robert" through the open door. Inside, Jimmy stood in the center of the room with a towel around his neck, holding a bottle of Jack Daniels and staring at the floor. Richard Cole sat bent over in a folding chair in the corner counting money in a brown suitcase.

"Australian," Frenchy said.

"Not a chance." I smirked. "Tell you what, you can be French, Frenchy."

"Fuck off."

An hour later the door was flung open. A massive figure filled the entire frame. Peter Grant, Zeppelin's manager. His swollen gut jutted out in the hallway. A ring of scraggly hair wrapped around the sides of his bald head and blended with a dark goatee. His voiced boomed.

"All of you. Get the fuck out of the way."

He lumbered through the crowd and Zeppelin and their entourage snaked behind him. Security guards fanned out around him, adding to the crush of bodies in the narrow hallway.

The four members of Led Zeppelin moved untouched in the center of it all. Jimmy and John Paul Jones wore sunglasses. John Bonham and Robert kept their heads down, trying not to make eye contact with anyone. The entire procession moved quickly down the hallway, charging like a herd of animals.

Me and Frenchy were sandwiched between the crowd and the wall. We swam through the crowd to keep up. I turned sideways to slip past a pair of groupies then bent to duck under the arm of a photographer holding his camera above the crowd. Zeppelin edged away from us up ahead.

"Come on, Patrick," Frenchy yelled from behind me. "We gotta get up there."

The crowd kept moving as I tried to maneuver around a

pear-shaped hippie in front of me. He was just too big. His wallet dangled from his back pocket, squeezed to the top by his flared jeans. I tugged the wallet loose and tossed it in front of him.

"Aw, shit," he howled. He dropped to his knees and scrambled to wrap a meaty hand around the wallet. I dodged to the right, grabbing a fistful of Frenchy's shirt and dragging him with me. The crowd behind us slammed into the hippie in a pile-up of hair and sweat.

We caught up with the main entourage and I shoved Frenchy toward Richard Cole.

"Get to it, Reginald!" I whispered to him.

"Mr. Cole," he stumbled nervously.

Richard Cole kept walking.

"Mr. Cole, my name is Reginald Chamberlain. I have a guitar that Mr. Page might be interested in."

"What is it?" Richard asked, keeping his eyes locked on the Civic Center's rear exit as we raced toward it.

"It's a nineteen sixty Telecaster. Great condition."

Richard cocked his head to the side and whispered to Jimmy, "Nineteen sixty Telecaster."

From behind his giant sunglasses, Jimmy Page jerked his head in the slightest of movements. I barely saw it. Richard turned back to Frenchy.

"Not interested."

"Really?" Frenchy stuttered. "But didn't Jimmy play a Fifty-eight Telecaster for the solo on 'Stairway to Heaven'?"

"I told you, he don't want it. Now piss off."

Frenchy looked back at me and shrugged. I waved my hand in the air, motioning for him to keep talking. I couldn't hear what they were saying. I walked on my tiptoes to see over the crowd. Frenchy said something and Jimmy's head spun toward him. He nodded rapidly.

Suddenly we were outside, launched from the back door of the Civic Center into the cool summer night. Zeppelin and their entourage slipped with military precision into a waiting black limo. Richard was the last one in. He stopped in front of Frenchy.

"Well? Where the fuck is it?"

"Where are you staying? I'll bring it to your hotel."

Richard climbed into the waiting limo. Something was wrong.

"There's no hotel." He laughed. "We're taking the jet back to New York tonight."

"But how will I get the guitar to you?" Frenchy pleaded.

"Bring it to New York this weekend. We're staying at the Drake Hotel until Sunday."

The limo driver slammed the door as I caught up with Frenchy.

"What the fuck just happened?" I asked.

"Um . . . I told them we also had a Fifty-eight Les Paul."

"What's that?" I asked.

"Listen, I'm sorry! I got nervous. I didn't know what to say."

"What the fuck are you talking about? What's a Fifty-eight Les Paul?"

"It's one of the rarest guitars in the world." Frenchy sighed.

"Where the fuck are we going to get one?" I shouted.

I couldn't believe it. I thought to myself, This can't get worse.

"Haven Street Pawnshop has one."

It was now worse.

The limo pulled away and I stared at the glowing taillights until they disappeared over the hill and moved toward the airport and the private jet waiting to take Zeppelin to New York. I tore the fake mustache off Frenchy's face but Zeppelin was too far away to hear him scream.

EIGHT

just another pawn

there are SOME PEOPLE AND PLACES THAT YOU JUST DON'T FUCK WITH EVEN IF YOU'RE THE DIRTIEST CROOK AROUND. BAIL BONDS OFFICES. GUN SHOWS. PAWNSHOPS. YEARS OF DEALING WITH THE MEANEST AND DEADLIEST ASSHOLES IN THE WORLD HAS LEFT MOST OPERATORS EVEN MEANER AND DEADLIER THAN THE CUSTOMERS. SCREWING AROUND WITH THEM IS JUST PLAIN STUPID.

In Baltimore, there was one person that you definitely didn't mess with: Backwoods Billy Harvick. Ten years ago, Backwoods Billy ran with a pack of motorcycle nuts. Guys with names like Jimmy "Two Bottles" and "Hairy" Garfield. They were animals. They stole anything, tore up everywhere they went and kicked the shit out of anyone. They would have been a real motorcycle gang if any of them had bothered to come up with a name.

One night after a ride, Backwoods Billy and his guys showed up at the Damn Tap, a beaten-down bar in Fell's

Point. They went wild. They terrorized the waitress, stole everything they could and broke everything else. Someone found a safe in the back room and started prying at it with a crowbar. When the owner stepped in, Backwoods Billy split his head with a socket wrench and dragged him out to the street. They laid him facedown in the gutter and Backwoods Billy ran over the poor guy's skull with his bike. Then they tore out of there.

The police busted him but couldn't prove anything. The bikers had their story sewn up. As they told it, the owner attacked Backwoods Billy and when the fight didn't go his way he ran out into the street, where he was creamed by a car.

"Happens all the time, Officer. Especially late at night. The roads are loaded with drunk drivers after the bars close. Hell, we're gambling with our lives riding our bikes that late, ya know?"

Backwoods Billy ended up with manslaughter. He got seven years and served five. He found Jesus in prison, gave up pills, got his GED and taught a Bible study class. When they let him out, he went straight back to the gang's clubhouse in Canton. He gathered up the old gang, gave them Bibles and christened them the Holy Ghosts.

They were still the same psychos, only now they wore a skull-and-cross patch. Nothing else had changed. They still sold pills, still knocked off stores, still beat the hell out of people. The only difference was that this time they didn't get busted. The few Holy Ghosts actually to see the inside of a courtroom always dodged serious time. They were blessed with a string of botched trials. Missing witnesses. Cops with foggy memories. Misplaced evidence. One miracle after another.

The newspapers ran photos of Backwoods Billy standing outside the courthouse, Bible in hand, praising Jesus and defending the misunderstood Holy Ghosts and all of their hard work for the community like their charity car wash and Christmas toy drive. The law couldn't touch him. He could fuck with you any way he wanted and get away with it.

The Holy Ghosts' main business was selling pills. Black Beauties. Yellow Jackets. Blue Devils. They invested in a few businesses around town: an auto garage, two tattoo parlors and their main operation—Haven Street Pawnshop.

If robbing a pawnshop was a death wish, then robbing one owned by Backwoods Billy and the Holy Ghosts was guaranteed suicide. This could only end badly. I pictured the four of us buried alive under fresh concrete. Frenchy figured we'd be dragged behind motorcycles.

And yet here we were, pulling into the back parking lot of the Haven Street Pawnshop. The squat brick building looked more like a bunker than a store. Thick iron bars covered the two small windows and a tiny neon sign blinked PAWN. The sun shimmered off a freshly waxed Cadillac parked alongside the building.

A glass jewelry case lined the right side of the store and ended at a stack of TVs in the corner. Piles of drills and other tools filled shelves along the back wall, their power chords dripping toward the dirty tile floor. Rows of guitars perched on stands next to tiny amps and keyboards along the left wall.

"Hey, Pete," the old man behind the counter said as we walked in.

"Hey, Dave," Frenchy said, waving.

Alex whispered into Frenchy's ear, "Your name ain't Pete. It's Frenchy. Don't forget it."

"Fuck you," Frenchy whispered back.

"How the hell does the guy behind the counter know you?" I asked.

"I come in here a lot." Frenchy shrugged.

"Need help with anything?" Dave asked.

"Nah. Just looking around. Thanks."

Me and Alex pretended to be interested in an old TV. Frenchy strummed on an acoustic guitar then put it back on a stand. Keith plunked at a keyboard. Down the aisle Frenchy picked up an electric guitar, plugged the chord into an amp and sat down on a stool. The amp buzzed and hummed as he inched the volume knob toward ten.

Frenchy tore into "Voodoo Chile." I recognized the riff just as he hurled into the main chords. The sound rattled everything in the store. Guitars vibrated on their stands. The glass counters rattled. Dave ran from behind the counter yelling something but the sound drowned out the words. He fumbled with earplugs, cramming them into his ears as he hurried toward us.

"Pete! Pete!" he shouted.

Frenchy didn't look up. He dipped his shoulder and launched into the solo. His hand leapt up the neck of the guitar then slid back down. He held a note and lay into the whammy bar, twisting the sound around the store. Dave grabbed the neck of the guitar and Frenchy stopped playing. It felt like the air had been sucked out of the room.

"Pete! Goddamn it! I told you to cut that shit out," Dave said.

"Sorry, Dave. Just showing my buddies some stuff." Frenchy shrugged. He turned the amp down lower then quietly played "Little Wing." I couldn't believe it. Frenchy was one hell of a guitar player.

"Damn, man," I said. "When'd you learn to play like that?"

"Just been playing a lot lately, I guess."

"All right, Frenchy," Alex said. He was getting anxious. "Where's this guitar?"

Frenchy looked across the store.

"I don't know. It's usually right there."

He pointed to an empty stand in a glass display case. If that guitar was gone we were all screwed.

"Hey, Dave. You finally sell the Fifty-eight Les Paul?" Frenchy shouted.

"Hell no." Dave laughed. "Nobody around here has enough money for a guitar like that. It's in the back office."

Keith named songs for Frenchy to play and somehow Frenchy knew most of them. Even some Sabbath. Alex and I wandered the store, scoping out the layout. I ran over the setup in my head. You couldn't come in through the front windows with those bars and all the traffic on the street outside. The side windows were small and high, making it too difficult to slip in and too hard to climb out in a hurry.

When Dave grabbed another guitar to jam with Frenchy, me and Alex peeked into the back office. A metal door stood out along the rear wall.

"That must lead to the alley," I said.

"No alarm. Looks like that's our way in."

"Drill out the hinges?"

Alex nodded.

"Shit, man," I said. "We don't know how to do that. This is tougher than anything we've ever pulled. And if we fuck it up, we're dead men. Backwoods Billy will kill all of us."

"I think we should ask Danny to help."

"Danny? He can't cross the street without getting arrested. No. That's a horrible idea. I'm never working with him again."

"I'm telling you, he could do this. And we'll be there to make sure he doesn't fuck it up."

It was a stupid idea but I didn't have a better one.

"All right. But you have to talk him into it. And don't tell him anything about Zeppelin. Just tell him we're doing this to rip off the guitar."

"When?" Alex asked.

"Might as well do it tonight."

Me and Alex never noticed Dave walking up behind us.

"You guys looking for the Fifty-eight?" Dave asked.

We both jumped. Dave grabbed a guitar case from behind a desk and we followed him back out into the store. The clasps on the Gibson case snapped open and Dave lifted the lid. The guitar was gorgeous. Oranges and reds and yellows swirled in the finish, and the silver pick-ups reflected light around the room.

"Gibson used to make the Les Paul in a gold color," Dave explained. "The Fifty-eight was the first year in the sunburst finish."

"That's such a sweet guitar, man." Keith nodded. "How much you selling it for?"

Dave laughed.

"Only seventeen hundred of these exist in the entire world. The guy who buys this beauty better come in here with a pretty big goddamn checkbook."

"Shit. I don't even have a checking account," Keith said with a shrug.

As we left Dave called out behind us. He held up the guitar.

"You sure none of you guys wanna take this?" He smiled.

Alex looked back.

"Not right now, man."

NINE
electric funeral

first, empty YOUR POCKETS. DUMP ANYTHING THAT MAKES NOISE. NO LOOSE CHANGE. NO KEYS. DON'T EVEN BOTHER WITH A WALLET. YOU DON'T NEED IT. IF IT FALLS OUT, YOU'RE FUCKED. NEVER CARRY IDENTIFICATION. MAKE UP A FAKE NAME AND USE THE SAME ONE EVERY TIME. SOMETHING EASY TO REMEMBER. ONE YOU KNOW YOU WON'T FUMBLE. I'M JOHN OSBOURNE, OZZY OSBOURNE'S REAL NAME.

Second, get a story. One that gets rid of cops fucking pronto. Nothing that might make them want to help you. You didn't lose your dog. Your car didn't break down. And it can't be something they can trace. You didn't just get out of a movie. You didn't just get off work. What are you doing out this late? You went for a walk to clear your head after a fight on the phone with a girlfriend. You didn't bother to bring your wallet.

Stick to the plan regardless of what falls in your lap. Don't risk going after something else no matter how tempting. Get what you came for and get out. One time, while Alex was climbing out of a house, I spotted a large bag in the backseat of the car. It looked like a camera bag or a small piece of luggage with cash or traveler's checks inside. A neighbor heard me break the window and called the cops. We barely got away. What was in the bag? Diapers.

Always plan on running. Double-tie your shoes. Don't wear clothes that make noise. That means no windbreakers. And be careful with hoods. They look suspicious. If you wear a hooded sweatshirt, make it a zip-up. Hoods make great handles for cops to grab when you're running. If you're lucky, you can unzip and leave him holding your hood and nothing else. If you do run, hit the backyards, not the streets. And don't worry about anyone else. You're on your own when they show. Pick a direction and run.

Almost a year had passed since the last time I was involved with anything like this but I still remembered the rules. Well, they weren't rules. Just simple shit that Alex and I worked out over the years. I went over them in my head as we sat around the kitchen table at Keith's house waiting on Danny. He was already half an hour late.

"I don't see why I have to come," Frenchy said.

"To make sure we get the right guitar," Alex argued.

"I already showed you which guitar."

"All that shit looks the same to me. Especially in the dark. Just point it out."

The front door creaked open and Danny slipped through. He tiptoed loudly across the living room. Me and Alex looked at each other and tried not to laugh. Danny sprung into the kitchen wearing a black sweatshirt, camouflage pants, black boots and a black stocking cap. He grabbed Keith in a headlock before Keith realized he was there.

"Whoa, boy!" Danny yelled. "You'd have been a dead man."

"Let go of me, asshole," Keith yelled, pulling on Danny's arm.

"You pussies are going to have to be sharper than that tonight," Danny told us. He wrestled with Keith. The kitchen chair fell with a crash.

"You see how quiet I was? You guys never heard me coming. I coulda killed ya. Learned that from an ex–Navy SEAL I met in the joint."

"We all heard you walk in, dumbass," Keith grunted.

"Yeah. You say that now."

Keith struggled to pry Danny's arm from around his neck. Danny let go with a shove, sending Keith flailing across the kitchen. Danny stood with his hands on his hips, a grin across his face. He straightened his stocking cap.

"Great outfit, G.I. Joe," I said.

Alex and Keith laughed. Danny leaned over the table.

"Fuck you, Patrick. You're learning from a master tonight. Let's go, kids!"

Danny turned and charged toward the front door. His clunky boot hooked in the carpeting and he stumbled across the living room. The door slammed and seconds later my car horn honked twice. We all looked at each other.

"Get a move on," he yelled.

On the way out I caught Alex's eye and shook my head.

"He'll be fine," he said to me. "Besides, he's the best at this shit. You know that."

"I'm pretty sure we could handle it better if we didn't have to babysit his dumb ass."

"I'll keep an eye on him."

We didn't talk on the way to the pawnshop. Sabbath's "Electric Funeral" played on the radio. One of the evilest riffs ever written. Everyone stared out the windows. When we got close, Danny told me to pull over at a gas station. The building was locked up for the night and the dark parking lot sat empty.

"Why are we stopping here?" I asked. I worried he planned to rob the gas station too.

"Alex, get out," he said, pointing into the blackness of the gravel lot.

"What the fuck for?" Alex answered.

"Get your ass over there and call the pawnshop."

"Why the fuck would he do that?" I stammered. Goddamn it, I thought, I knew I shouldn't have let Alex talk me into this. This idiot was going to get us all arrested. "We're going to the pawnshop. Why the hell would he call there?"

"He's going to call it then leave the phone off the fucking hook. That way it keeps ringing."

"What's the fucking point of that?" Alex said. "They're closed."

Danny took a long drag on his cigarette then blew smoke from the corner of his mouth.

"If the phone's still ringing when we get there, we know no one's inside and it's safe to go in."

That made sense. Everyone relaxed a bit. It sounded pretty smart, actually, and when Alex climbed back into the car and told us it was still ringing I felt a bit more confident that we might actually pull this off.

Haven Street Pawnshop sat in the darkness of a tiny parking lot. Cars streamed past on the street out front. I shut off the headlights and pulled up into the alley. I found a parking spot just far enough away from the rear door not to raise suspicion. The phone was still ringing inside.

At the back door to the store, Danny handed Keith a bright red crowbar then leaned against the hood of my car. Keith fumbled the bar, nearly dropping it, and Frenchy lunged forward to catch it before it clattered to the ground.

"Damn it, Keith," Danny hissed. "What the hell's wrong with you?"

"Sorry," Keith mumbled.

Danny pushed his face into Keith's.

"You nervous or something?" he asked.

"Yeah. I guess so."

Danny stepped closer, causing Keith to move backward toward the door behind him.

"What are you so nervous about?" Danny asked.

"I'm not really that nervous. My hands are just sweaty."

"Which is it, man? Are you nervous or are your hands just sweaty?" Danny moved closer to Keith. "How do I know you aren't an undercover cop?"

"For fuck's sake, Danny," I groaned. "You've known Keith his whole damn life. Let's get this over with."

"No!" Danny said, not taking his eyes off Keith. "We need to find out what he's hiding."

"Keith," I said, cutting Danny off. "Open that fucking door."

The metal door fit tight into the frame and Keith struggled to wedge the jimmy bar in. Danny wrestled the bar from Keith's hands then twisted it into place. He stepped back, looked at Keith and pointed at the bar. Keith grabbed the bar with both hands and threw his weight backward when his grip, sweaty with nerves, slipped from the bar. He stumbled backward in slow motion before collapsing on the gravel parking lot in a tangle of limbs and dirty hair.

Alex choked back a stoner giggle and I covered my mouth to keep from erupting. Keith groaned softly, lying facedown in the gravel. He rolled over on his back and wiped tiny rocks from his bleeding elbow. Alex stood over him laughing. He kicked Keith lightly in the ribs and told him to get up. Frenchy looked up and down the alley, searching for an excuse to run.

"All right, you morons," Danny said. "Let's just do this and get out of here."

The crowbar dangled from the door frame where it was wedged in the paint. Danny grabbed the end with both hands and pried the door a few inches away from the frame, then twisted the bar to hold it open. He walked over to my car, leaned in the window to pop the trunk, then pulled the car-jack from inside. He stepped forward and wedged the edge of the jack into the opening. A cigarette dangled from the corner of his mouth as his arms pumped up and down on the handle. The jack rose, separating the heavy steel door from the frame with a loud groan until the frame shattered and the door sprung backward.

Frenchy peered nervously around the open doorway and into the dark store until Danny shoved him out of the way. Danny strode through the shattered door frame into the rear office and around an oversized desk covered with papers and folders.

"Let's go."

Streetlights lit the store floor and reflected off the glass display cases. The neat rows of guitars looked like tombstones spread out in front of us. We stood against the back wall and took it all in. Danny let out a soft whistle.

"Let's just get the guitar and get out of here," Frenchy said.

"What's the hurry, Frenchy?" Alex asked.

"No. Fuck you, Alex. We're getting this guitar and getting the fuck out."

Alex cupped his hands and lit a cigarette. He turned his head and let out a thick cloud then poked at Frenchy with the glowing cigarette as he spoke.

"All I'm saying is you helped us out with this thing. It's only fair that you get something for yourself too. Grab a guitar. Shit, man, as long as we're here."

Frenchy wrestled with the idea. The struggle didn't last long.

"Yeah. Maybe I will. You guys did drag me into this."

"Me and Frenchy will grab the guitar. You guys watch the alley." I pulled Frenchy into the darkness before anyone could argue.

While Frenchy picked out a guitar, I prowled the store looking for the '58 Les Paul. It wasn't on a stand with the other guitars or behind the keyboards. I was inspecting a stack of guitar cases on the floor by the power tools when Alex snuck up behind me.

"Looking for this?" he asked. He held the black hard-shell guitar case with the '58 Les Paul inside. "I found it sitting in the back office."

"Sweet." I sighed. "Where are Danny and Keith? You can't let Danny out of your sight. He'll fuck this up."

"Don't worry. They're out back loading the car."

"Loading the car with what?" I snapped.

"The safe from the back room. Danny thought we should take it. There's probably a ton of cash in there."

"Jesus, man," I growled. "We just came for the guitar. Now you guys are stealing the fucking safe?"

I hurried toward the back office and found Keith drinking a beer and rummaging through a tiny refrigerator next to the desk. He poked his head over the door and bit into a chicken drumstick.

"Keith! What the fuck? You're supposed to be watching the fucking alley."

"I got hungry."

A mangled chicken leg hung out of his mouth.

"That's really gross, man. You have no idea how old that is."

"Is thwat blad?" he chewed.

"Yeah, it's bad. You're gonna get sick."

He shrugged and swallowed.

"Aw, shit! Look what I found." Danny giggled from behind Keith.

Keith turned toward Danny then spun back around and slammed into me. He dropped his chicken leg and shoved to get past me and out the back door into the alley. Danny stood behind him pointing a pistol at me.

"Put that shit away, man," I said as I backed up.

"Yeah, Danny," Alex said, holding up his hands. "Don't fuck around. We're getting out of here."

Danny grinned. He leveled the barrel toward the wall.

"Enough bullshit, Danny," I said. "Put it down."

"Fuck you, Patrick. What are you gonna do about it?"

"All right. All right," Alex said, taking Danny's arm. "Take it easy. Let's get in the car. Patrick, you grab Frenchy."

Frenchy stood in the darkness strumming an electric guitar. Even unplugged I could make out the chords to "Ruby Tuesday" ringing across the silent store.

"Is that the one you want?" I asked him.

"I'm not sure. I really like this Fender but as long as it's free I might as well get something really expensive. Or maybe I should take an acoustic?"

"Grab three guitars. I don't care. Let's just get out of here."

Frenchy started to move. His face looked strange, lit by red and blue lights.

Shit. Red and blue lights.

"Fuck! Cops!" I yelled.

Frenchy dropped the guitar and sprinted toward the back door. The front door rattled open and flashlights filled the store. A voice boomed out behind me: "Freeze right there, asshole!"

I bolted across the back office, doing my best to dodge the swirling flashlights. I slammed the heavy security door to the office behind me and dropped the security bar. Fists pounded against the steel door as I sprinted out the back and into the alley.

The glowing red taillights of my car looked miles away. The metal edges of the safe jutted from my trunk and the back end of the car sagged with the weight. A knotted shoestring held the trunk lid closed.

Danny sat behind the wheel with his arm across the seat and his head turned looking back at me. Alex sat in the passenger seat talking to Danny. Even without hearing him I knew what he was saying: "Wait." The car revved and my hands fumbled for the door handle as Danny floored the gas pedal, spraying a rooster tail of gravel. Frenchy and Keith stared out the back window as the car tore down the alley away from me. I waved my arms over my head hoping they would stop. Red and blue lights rounded the corner behind me.

I picked a direction and ran.

TEN

bats

i woke UP SHIRTLESS AND SWEATING. SOMETHING STABBED INTO MY SIDE AND I ROLLED OVER, PEELED A BOTTLE CAP OFF MY SKIN AND HURLED IT TOWARD THE CORNER. A HAND KNOCKED ON MY BEDROOM DOOR.

"Patrick. Are you up?" my mother asked from the other side.

"I'm up," I moaned, straightening my twisted boxer shorts. I opened the door. She wore bright yellow shorts and a flowered top, and held a spatula in her hand.

"I made breakfast," she said. "Are you going to join us?"

Her eyes trailed down my face and across my bare chest. My stomach dropped when I remembered the tattoo I'd gotten in New York City. I slumped against the door frame to hide it and faked a yawn, but she had already spotted it.

"What have you done?" she said. Her lipsticked mouth hung open.

"It's nothing."

"No. It's something, mister. It's terrible. Why would you do that to your body?"

"Okay. It's something."

"Don't get smart with me," she mumbled. The angry tone chugged to a halt in her throat and she suddenly seemed less threatening. The anger downshifted into something else but I wasn't sure what.

"Your father is going to have a heart attack if he sees this," she whispered. Her wide eyes met mine. We were suddenly partners in a horrible crime.

"Here he comes. Get some clothes on."

She shoved me backward into my room and I lunged to pull the door closed as I fell over a pile of clothes and an old skateboard.

My mother slipped me a knowing look as I sat down at the kitchen table. My father was talking about the fire department again. He was a fireman and being a fireman was his entire life. It went beyond dedication to straight brainwashing. He didn't know anything except being a fireman. Music. Movies. Sports. World affairs. Nothing. The only politics he followed were local and only because they might have affected the firehouse, like with a budget cut or new equipment being bought for another station in town before his.

My sister and I were his only connection to the rest of the world. If a conversation turned to anything other than firefighting, he threw us out there like a goddamn lifeline. Talk about a new movie and he'd say that his daughter saw it and didn't like it. Bring up the World Series and he'd tell you how his lazy-ass son quit Little League.

It was the only way he could talk about anything other than

the firehouse. And he could steer any conversation toward firefighting. Pick a topic and he would turn it into a rant about the VFW's fire code violations that got overlooked by the chief as a favor to a buddy. He and his work were the center of any conversation. You couldn't win. I'd stopped trying years earlier.

"I bet you don't get breakfasts like this in New York City, Pat," my mother said.

"Nope," I said. "This is great."

"Are you eating enough? You look skinny."

"I eat a lot, actually. Usually leftovers from whatever catering job I worked the night before."

"So the job is fun?" she asked.

"It's all right. I work with some cool guys. Plus, I get to be backstage at all the concerts."

"How exciting," she said, grinning.

"You know who I met the other night? Bette Midler."

My mother gasped and clutched her chest.

"No! Did you really? What was she like?"

"We were all backstage at Radio City Music Hall when she came out of her dressing room, walked over to the food table, looked at me and said, 'Where the fuck is the cranberry juice I asked for?' "

We both laughed until my father spoke up.

"You guys better be keeping those tables clear of the fire exits. Some dumb rock star leaves a lit cigarette in the dressing room and that place goes up, you'll all die trying to get out."

I stood up and dumped my plate in the sink.

"I'll keep that in mind, Pop," I said as I slipped out the front door.

My car sat crooked in the street in front of my parents' house. Keys in the ignition. Guitar and safe gone. Gas tank empty. A note under the windshield wiper.

*THANKS FOR LETTING US BARROW YOUR CAR. WE
DIDN'T HAVE ANY MONIE FOR GAS. DANNY*

"Whole Lotta Love" played on the radio as I pulled over to the curb in front of Frenchy's house. I climbed out of the car just as Robert Plant started groaning about giving me his love. What an awful fucking song.

The sun set and I kicked a bottle as I crossed the street. Frenchy lived in his parents' basement. Bare concrete floor and walls. Frenchy dressed it up with a smelly rug, a sofa he found in the alley and some posters. It wasn't so bad. Through the window I could see him, wearing a faded Who T-shirt and jeans, playing guitar on the couch in front of the flicker from a TV sitting on a milk crate.

"What's this? A high school reunion?" He smiled as he let me in. It was our private joke. Keith and Alex dropped out of school so me and Frenchy were the only people we knew who graduated. To us, it was a high school reunion whenever we were together.

"Just out seeing what you're up to," I told him.

"Nothing. Playing guitar. Watching TV."

I poured myself into Frenchy's couch. He hesitated for a second then spoke.

"Hey, man," he said. "Sorry about last night. I—"

"Don't worry about it," I interrupted. "I know it was Danny. What happened?"

"I told him to wait. Just so you know."

"I know."

"So where's the safe and the guitar?"

"You're sitting on it," he answered, pointing to the couch.

I bent over, looking at the tattered couch underneath me.

"The guitar is under there," he explained. "Danny and Alex took the safe."

"Where did they take it?"

"I don't know. They dropped me off with the guitar first. They didn't say where they were going after that."

Frenchy opened two beers and handed me one.

"So what's the plan now?" he asked, leaning forward. "Are we going to go to New York?"

"Of course," I answered, sipping my beer.

"I just don't know if we can pull it off," Frenchy said, staring at the floor.

"It's simple, man. We bring him the Les Paul and, while you're in there, me, Keith and Alex will grab the money. Then we get out of there."

"I don't know, man. I'm starting to get worried."

"What are you worried about?" I asked him. "We're just a couple of guys trying to sell Jimmy Page a guitar. We haven't done anything wrong."

"We're trying to sell him a guitar that we just stole from one of the biggest psychos in Baltimore!"

"Yeah, well, there's that."

Frenchy clicked off the TV and put a record on the turntable. Frenchy was the only person I knew as obsessed with music as me. He liked raw rock 'n' roll, usually British stuff. The Animals and the Who and obscure stuff I didn't even know. He turned me on to tons of new stuff like the Stooges and MC5. His record collection lined the walls. Hundreds of LPs bought with money he made working at the Record Barn. The rest were probably stolen. He dropped the needle on the record and stood grinning at me.

"What?" I asked him.

"Just listen."

"What am I listening to?"

"You'll dig this."

The song kicked in. Loud R&B guitar, swirling drums, hand claps. It sounded fucking great. A raspy voice howled, *I ain't foolin'... Hey woman you need coolin'.* I knew the song but it took me a second to place it. It was Zeppelin's "Whole Lotta Love," just different. Cooler.

"Holy shit!" I sat up. "Is this someone covering 'Whole Lotta Love'?"

"Nope." Frenchy grinned. "This is the song Zeppelin stole it from."

"No fucking way!" I laughed. "This is ridiculous. Let me see that jacket."

"It's the Small Faces 'You Need Loving.' Came out three years before Zeppelin's version."

"The singer sounds exactly like Plant!"

"Yeah. They stole the whole vocal idea."

"Goddamn." I shook my head. "Just another reason to hate them."

"Well, the Small Faces took it from Muddy Waters. Zeppelin just stole their version of it," Frenchy said.

"And the entire fucking sound."

"Yeah." He laughed. He sat on the floor and dug through a crate of records. "Jimmy Page ripped off the beginning of 'Stairway to Heaven' from this band Spirit. I heard 'Dazed and Confused' is lifted from some folksinger."

"Fucking con artists."

"They're still amazing. Everyone borrows, man. That's just music."

"Oh, don't give me that shit. This is outright theft. They totally stole these songs."

"They took the same elements that everyone else used and did it better. Look, if I put peanut butter and jelly on bread it's not the most original sandwich but you'd still eat it."

"I don't even know what the fuck that means."

We went on like that for a while, talking music and listening to records. We could do that for hours. It felt good to hang with Frenchy and not worry about anything except if the Stones put out better albums without Brian Jones (they did) or if the Animals were better than the Who (sometimes). Eventually the beer ran out and I headed home. It was late and I was hungry so I stopped for a burger.

My car sat alone in a corner spot at the back of the parking lot as I left the restaurant with a bag of food. A Black Sabbath eight-track slipped to the floor and I stretched across the front seat to grab it then crammed it into the player. I fumbled with my keys and finally fit them in the ignition. That's when I heard something metal tap against the window.

I didn't even turn all the way around. All I needed to see was that ring knocking against the glass. That giant silver skull ring with a bullet slug buried in its forehead. The ring was so big it covered up the entire section of his middle finger including one letter of a tattoo that ran across the knuckles of his hand. It didn't matter. I knew the black ink spelled out *P-A-I-N*. I didn't have to see the other hand to know it said *L-O-S-S*. It hit me that I was fucked in the worst possible way.

"Get out of the car, son," he said.

I looked through my dirty car window. He wore a wifebeater tank top underneath a leather motorcycle jacket and denim vest covered in patches. His greasy red hair hung past his shoulders and tangled with a kinky beard half a foot long. A huge tattoo crawled up his neck beneath it. At the base of his throat he'd tattooed a picture of a jackalope, an imaginary rabbit with antlers that turns up on postcards from Texas. The head sat mounted on a plaque and the tattooed antlers stretched up his throat and stopped just underneath his chin. The banner tattooed around it said, BACKWOODS.

This was Backwoods Billy Harvick.

I slunk from the car. Someone struck me from behind and

a thick hand in a fingerless leather glove squeezed around my throat. When I tried to stand a heavy boot rocketed into my shins and knocked me to the ground then stood on the side of my head, grinding my face into the parking lot. Gravel bit into my cheek. I turned my eyes to look up at Backwoods Billy.

"You see this bike?" he said. His greasy finger pointed at the motorcycle. Despite all of his filth, the bike was spotless. The high handlebars, the long chopper forks and chrome tailpipes gleamed in the dark.

"There was a time in my life when that bike was all I had to live for. That was it. I didn't have a home or a woman. No job. No family. That bike was it. You know what that does to ya?"

I started to say something but couldn't think. Visions of that giant bike rolling over my head played in my mind. He kept going.

"It makes ya think human life is cheap. You don't care nothing about your own life so you don't care nothing about nobody else's. Back then we wouldn't be talking like this. I would have already killed ya for what ya done to me."

My heart stumbled and the strength drained out of my legs. I raced through my brain trying to figure out how Backwoods Billy knew we'd robbed the Haven Street Pawnshop. I stared at the ground.

"Lucky for you I don't act like that no more. I've got God in my life now and a wife and kids to look after. But that don't mean I'm gonna let you get away with what you done." He pointed at me. "As the Bible says, 'Know this, that if the good man of the house had known in what watch the thief would come, he would have watched, and would not have suffered his house to be broken up.' "

"Is that what you think I did? Broke into your house?" I talked so fast that I tripped over my own words. It sounded like three people speaking at once. "Because I didn't. I wouldn't do that. You must be thinking of someone—"

"Shut up, son," he said. "Is this your car?"

"Yeah."

"This is the car my partner saw parked in the alley behind my pawnshop last night." He nodded to the person standing on my skull. The foot let up enough for me to turn my head to see the enormous bald man dressed in black jeans, motorcycle boots and a black leather vest crossing his bulging arms over his bare chest. He leaned down toward me and stared from behind dark sunglasses. My own frantic face peered back at me from the reflection in the lenses.

"You broke into my business last night and stole something very valuable to me," Billy said.

"This is just a huge misunderstanding," I said. "Someone obviously did something very fucking stupid. I can get the guitar back. Just give me some time."

"Guitar?" He grinned. "Hell, I don't care about no old guitar. That's Dave's shit. I'm talking about my safe, boy."

The safe. Fucking Danny.

"I'll get it back. I swear to you."

He leaned against his bike and pulled at his beard with a tattooed hand swollen with scars. I stared at the giant skull ring. He looked up at the sky. His partner stood nearby and Billy smiled at him. I held my breath. Finally he said something.

"Son, what you stole from me is very important and I need it back. So I'm gonna give you a chance to return it. Now I know I don't need to give you no deadline. I expect it to be brought back to me as fast as fucking possible. You know that. And believe me, boy, you'll know when I've run out of patience."

"I understand."

He crouched down and bent his head to put his face in mine.

"If you think I'm joking, you little shit, remember Samuel 22:38: 'I have pursued mine enemies and destroyed them and not turned away until I had consumed them. And I have consumed them and wounded them that they could not arise. They are fallen under my feet,' " he preached.

He stood up and turned to his partner.

"Okay, Rabbit. Let's give it to him."

Two meaty hands squeezed around my throat and jerked me to my feet. The force cocked my head backward and arched my back. The toes of my shoes scraped the ground. They're gonna beat the shit out of me, I thought. This was Backwoods Billy's warning to let me know that the Holy Ghosts were not fucking around. The empty parking lot stretched in every direction but I didn't even think about running. There wasn't a chance. As he walked closer, I stared at that big skull ring. He stopped and stuck out a tattooed arm. A tiny red Bible sat in the palm of his hand.

"Son, is God in your life?" Billy asked me. He pushed his face into mine.

"Well, I, uh . . ." I couldn't breathe.

"What you need to do, boy, is study the Bible and stay clean. Take this."

The monster behind me let go of my neck. I bent over gasping for air and rubbing my throat. Backwoods Billy dropped the Bible into my hand.

"Do you like Led Zeppelin?" he asked, swinging a leg over his motorcycle.

"Hell no," I choked.

It was instinct. I really didn't.

He nodded.

"That Jimmy Page is a devil worshiper and he's polluting kids' minds with that stuff."

I nodded and moved toward my car.

"The real stairway to heaven is right there in that little book, son. Rock 'n' roll is the devil's music."

"I don't even listen to rock," I lied, shutting my car door and rolling down the window. "I like Johnny Cash."

"There's hope for you yet, son." He smiled.

I turned the key in the ignition. Black Sabbath roared from the speakers: *"Look into my eyes you will see who I am / My name is Lucifer, please take my hand."*

The volume knob slipped from my hand so I jerked the eight-track from the player and threw it on the floor. I couldn't look at Backwoods Billy. I didn't want to see his reaction. I closed my eyes and rested my forehead on the cool steering wheel. I glanced over when I heard them kick-start their bikes with a roar of noise. Backwoods Billy scowled at me as he revved his bike. Then he wrenched the throttle and the two bikes streaked across the empty parking lot like giant bats disappearing into the night.

ELEVEN

no fun

lynyrd skynyrd BLASTED FROM THE BACK ROOM AT KEITH'S HOUSE. I HEARD THE MUSIC FROM THE STREET AS I WALKED FROM WHERE I'D PARKED UP THE BLOCK. KEITH HAD TOLD EVERYONE TO SCATTER THE CARS AROUND THE NEIGHBORHOOD TO MAKE IT LESS OBVIOUS THERE WAS A PARTY HERE. NO ONE LISTENED.

Sweaty bodies crowded together dancing and talking. The music played nearly too loud to talk over. Keith yelled my name. He was shirtless and struggled to pull himself up from the couch. Long greasy hair stuck to his face. He threw a sweaty arm around me. I wished him a happy birthday and handed him the bottle of vodka I'd stolen from the liquor store around the corner.

"Thanks, man," he slurred.

"How did you talk your mom into this?" I asked.

"I told her she didn't have to buy me anything. Just get out of the house for the night. She would have gone to the bar anyway."

It's not like a party could hurt anything. Keith and his mom didn't own much. They had lived in the house since me and Keith were ten and his mother still hadn't bought any furniture. The front room was entirely empty. Even the walls were bare. There was a nicked-up table in the kitchen that Keith's grandma gave them and in the back room a brown leather couch with stuffing bursting out and a tiny black-and-white TV. A photo of Keith from grade school hung crooked in the hallway. Keith's room contained a few piles of clothes, two boxes of comic books and an overflowing ashtray on the floor next to a mattress.

"Where's Danny?" I asked him.

"I think he's in the kitchen."

I moved toward the kitchen and scanned the room for Danny but didn't see him. I grabbed a beer in the kitchen, drank it too fast while talking to a chubby girl I went to school with and then opened another beer. Keith grabbed me and we did a shot of tequila together. The tequila kicked in. Someone played "Fortunate Son" and I started feeling all right. Earlier in the day I had called Alex and warned him about Backwoods Billy. We agreed to talk to Danny. I found Alex by the fridge.

"Where the fuck is Danny?" I asked.

"He'll be here," he said. He looked nervous. We stood there watching the crowd. "Have you seen Frenchy? The Frenchy Show is on tonight."

It was our name for those rare nights when Frenchy got completely drunk and out of control. It usually involved dancing. Sometimes nudity.

"Brown Sugar" started and I spotted Frenchy dragging a skinny blonde in a white dress toward the center of the room to dance. He wore a loud collared shirt unbuttoned, exposing his skinny chest. The girl towered over him and he was wasted and leaning too far forward to talk to her as they danced. A few times he lost his balance and fell into her, nearly knocking her down. He grabbed her arm and steadied himself then laughed. When the song ended they walked over.

"Guys, you gotta meet Sara," he panted. We all nodded at her. The stereo kicked into "You Really Got Me" and Frenchy struck a pose, throwing his head back and pointing toward the ceiling. He spun his arm in a few windmills on an invisible guitar then danced away from Sara and into the crowd. She giggled then turned to me.

"If you're not going to dance you can hold this," she barked. Her arm shot toward me and poked me in the chest with a leather purse. It looked expensive. The purse fell into my arms and she disappeared.

"What the fuck was that?" I asked Alex. He laughed.

"That's a woman who is used to ordering people around," he said.

We both stood there staring at her. Alex finished a cigarette and flicked the burning butt into the crowd.

"Well, what's she got?" he asked.

He unzipped the purse and pulled out her wallet. He crammed a wad of cash into his pocket and then held up a small camera.

"Want it?"

"No thanks," I said.

Alex poured the rest of his beer inside before zipping it back up. He chucked the purse on the floor next to the couch.

A girl's voice yelled from the kitchen, "Keep your fucking hands off me, you asshole!"

A male voice shouted back at her but I couldn't hear it over the music. I pushed toward the kitchen.

"Oh, I'm no fun?" the female voice shouted. "Fuck yourself. How's that for fun?"

As I shoved my way into the kitchen a tall girl in a green sundress pushed through the crowd going in the opposite direction.

"That asshole just grabbed my ass," she said to her friend as we passed.

Danny had arrived.

I found him standing on the far side of the kitchen table. He wore a dingy T-shirt from Tony's Pizza that read, "If you like my meatballs, you'll love my sausage." A bottle of Jim Beam dangled in the fingers of his right hand and he held a can of Pepsi in the left. He alternated swigs from each. First a mouthful of Jim, then a swallow of soda. A white-trash whiskey and Coke. He swayed a bit as I walked over.

"Danny. I need to talk to you."

"Patrick!" He leaned in to whisper but talked loudly. "There's a lot of pussy here."

He slapped me on the back.

"Sure is, man," I replied.

His eyes roamed over the people at the party. Judging by the whiskey missing from the bottle and the slur in his speech, I put Danny somewhere between drunk and really fucking drunk.

"Listen, Danny. We gotta return that safe."

"What do you mean?" he answered, not looking at me.

"Backwoods Billy wants his safe back. He knows what happened."

He stared out at the crowd and didn't say anything.

"You have to give it to me. We have to give it back to him."

"No can do, amigo," he said smugly, taking a hard swallow of whiskey, chased by a swallow of soda.

"You don't have a fucking choice, man." I tried to sound calm and reasonable. "He saw the car. He knows you have it."

"No. He thinks you have it." He jabbed a finger in my face.

"He wants the safe back and we're going to give it to him."

"Can't do it." Danny shrugged.

"Why not? Where is it?"

"I don't have it."

Slug of whiskey. Slug of Pepsi.

"Well, who the fuck does?" I asked. Danny looked away.

Alex's head popped over the crowd, looking for us. He found us standing against the wall.

"So are we getting the safe back from Boogie?" Alex asked. Danny looked annoyed.

"Yeah. We are," I answered.

I stared at Danny. He took another drink of whiskey, long and hard, and didn't bother with the soda.

"It ain't that easy, kiddies," he grimaced. "I made a deal with him. If he opens it, he gets a cut of whatever's inside."

"Well, that deal is off," I said. "We're not opening it and he doesn't get anything."

"You gonna tell him that?" Danny grinned. He looked away and laughed.

"Who's Boogie?" I asked Alex.

"Danny's buddy. He's a safecracker."

"We'll find him tomorrow and get it back," I said.

"Are you not fucking listening to me, Patrick?" Danny said, turning on me, his eyes read with anger and booze. "You're not getting it back. Boogie won't just hand it over to you. Once he cracks that fucker, I want what's inside. Boogie wants what's inside. And Alex wants what's inside. Right, Alex?"

Alex shrugged. Danny looked irritated.

"Why are you doing this?"

"I'm doing this because I need to give the safe back to Billy before he kills us all," I shouted.

Danny rolled his eyes and took a long pull from the whiskey bottle.

"We're giving it back, Danny. And that's that."

Danny grabbed my throat in one sloppy thrust. Alex jumped between us. We struggled together, a triangle of sweaty bodies all grunting and pulling in different directions. I swung and my fist careened off the side of Danny's head.

"I know kung fu, motherfucker!" Danny yelled, flailing with one arm. His feet tangled and he fell backward, pulling me and Alex down on top of him. He landed flat on his back on the kitchen floor with a grunt. My forehead ricocheted off the bridge of his nose.

"Aww, shit," he groaned.

Legs stood over me and from the corner of my eye I saw Keith yanking on Danny's arm.

"Break it up!" Keith yelled.

We all separated. Danny stood up and straightened his shirt then bent to pick up his bottle of Jim Beam. Blood snaked down the side of his nose. He stared at me for a second and then left, kicking the door open with a dirty boot.

Alex turned to me.

"He's just drunk. He knows you're right. I'll talk to him tomorrow."

I nodded and picked my beer bottle up off the floor.

"Let's get a beer and have some fun," he said. "There's a lot of pussy here."

"Yeah," I told him. "That's what I've heard."

TWELVE

the new york fucking giants

"**boogie's a** GODDAMN GENIUS," DANNY SAID THE NEXT DAY AS WE DROVE PAST THE HIGH SCHOOL AND AROUND THE BOWLING ALLEY. I DIDN'T KNOW WHAT TO EXPECT WHEN I PICKED HIM AND ALEX UP BUT ALL THE BULLSHIT FROM LAST NIGHT SEEMED TO HAVE BLOWN OVER. ALEX MUST HAVE TALKED HIM DOWN. DANNY WAS A BIT HUNGOVER BUT LOOSE AND RELAXED, CHATTING AWAY IN THE FRONT SEAT. A SNOOPY BAND-AID COVERED THE CUT ON HIS NOSE.

"Tell Patrick what Boogie was locked up for," Alex said, leaning up from the backseat. "You'll love this, Patrick. It's your kinda scheme."

"Get this." Danny grinned. "Boogie is this poor black kid. Smart as fuck. And he's big. He was born big. Every year football coaches begged Boogie to play but that ain't him. He was always into music. He can play anything—drums, guitar, piano. He didn't want to play football and hurt his hands and fuck up his music career."

"Makes sense," I said.

"He gets a job at this music store selling instruments and jewelry and shit. One time the owner went on vacation and the soda machine broke while he was gone. Boogie's too lazy to put a sign on it so people keep plugging in money. When they complain to him that it doesn't work he tells them they'll have to come back next week for a refund when the owner gets back. Nobody does."

"Really?" I asked.

"Would you go all the way across town for ten cents you lost in a fucking soda machine?"

"I guess not." I shrugged.

"So Boogie gets this idea. He and a buddy pool all their money and buy a bunch of soda and candy machines. They stick them outside Laundromats, magazine shops, movie theaters. The thing is, none of the machines work. People put in money and don't get shit. They don't know how to get a refund so they just give up. Once a month, Boogie and his buddy come by and clean out all the cash. And because the machines don't actually work, they're pulling in free money with no overhead."

"That is pretty goddamn clever."

"Hell yeah, it is." Danny grinned. "Shoot. I need to get a setup like that. That's fucking smart."

"It wasn't that smart. He did get busted, didn't he?"

"Well, yeah," Danny huffed. "Only because some chickenshit movie theater manager called the cops. They jumped him when Boogie came to collect."

"How long was he in?"

"Just three months. Shit, really nothing."

"What does he do now?"

"Not much. Lives out in this big house in Cherry Hill and works on his music. He's got a band."

"And he knows how to open a safe?"

"Hell yeah," Danny said, filling the car with a giant smoke cloud. "I told ya he's smart. He knows how to do all kinds of shit."

"Has he got it open yet?" Alex asked from the backseat.

"Not yet but he's working on it." Danny sounded annoyed and turned to face Alex. "Damn. Don't you trust me to take care of this shit?"

"I do," Alex said, sitting back. "I do."

"It doesn't matter," I said. "We're not opening it. We're getting it back from Boogie."

"We'll see about that." Danny smirked.

We barreled along the Washington Parkway. The businesses thinned out and soon we wound through used-car dealerships and run-down gas stations. Clusters of shabby apartment buildings huddled in threes and fours around sprawling parking lots dotted with burned-out cars and weed patches.

We wound along Cherry Hill Road until Danny told me to turn off on a narrow road leading through a small cluster of houses. A group of kids playing basketball in the street moved slowly to the side of the road and stared into the windows as we passed. The road kinked left but Danny pointed for me to keep straight into a gravel parking lot next to a beat-up yellow house tucked in the corner under a tree. All of the windows were closed even though the temperature lingered in the nineties. A tattered blue couch sat on concrete blocks in the front yard next to a rusted charcoal grill.

Danny said something to me and Alex as we walked toward the front door but I couldn't make out a word of it over the music exploding from the house. Tight funk drumming locked into step with a chicken-scratch guitar. Windows and doors rattled as the music pushed the old house to the verge of bursting.

Danny pounded on the screen door but the music washed

out the sound. I sat down on the step and Danny walked to the front of the house to rap on a basement window.

"They're pretty good, eh?" Alex asked me.

"Yeah, they are. Sounds like Sly Stone."

"Definitely. Figured out what you're going to say to Boogie?"

"I'll just tell him what happened." I sighed. "I'm sure he doesn't want any trouble with the Holy Ghosts either."

The music stopped and Danny dove to his knees in the dirt to beat on the window, burning himself with a cigarette in the process.

"Shit!" he yelped. "Hey, Boogie! Open up!"

A deep voice in the house said something and heavy foot-steps stomped up creaky basement steps. As the door opened, Danny pushed past us up the steps, brushing dirt off his jeans.

Boogie filled the entire door frame; his giant red button-up shirt took up most of the view. He dabbed sweat from his head with a white towel hanging around his neck then ducked to angle a towering Afro through the doorway and poke his puffy face outside.

"What's up, Danny?"

"Nothing, Boogie. Just stopped by to talk a second."

"Cool."

Inside the house, cables snaked along the hallways, up and down the stairs, and tangled with table legs and other furni-ture. A microphone on a stand stood alone in a tiny bathroom off a kitchen cluttered with beer bottles and empty pizza boxes. Guitar cases, dusty mixing boards and an old organ sur-rounded another sagging couch in the living room. A sawed-off shotgun lay in the sink. Boogie dropped into a chipped wooden chair in the kitchen. It creaked under his weight.

"So what's up?" he asked slowly in a deep voice.

"Well, uh . . ." Danny stammered. "I just wanted to see how things were going with the safe?"

"I'm working on it."

"Is it here?"

"Nah," Boogie said, giving Danny a suspicious look. "It's at my shop."

The basement door opened and a short, marble-shaped black guy ambled into the room. He held drumsticks in one meaty hand and rubbed the back of his neck with the other, creating rings of fat under his tucked-in chin. A short Afro radiated around his head.

"That's our drummer Johnny Paycheck," Boogie said.

"You mean like the country singer?" I blurted out. Boogie laughed. A thick grin grew across his face.

"Maaaannn," Johnny hissed in a high-pitched voice. "I was using this shit before that corny redneck motherfucker."

"I take it you don't like country music?" I asked.

"I'm from the South, man. I love country music. Hank Williams. Ernest Tubb. My mama played all that shit. Some of them country cats can really play."

"So Johnny Paycheck is just a stage name?"

"Yeah." He nodded. "For the band."

"What's the band called?" Alex asked. Behind him Boogie whistled and shook his head.

"See," Johnny said. "That's another problem right there. I know what I want to call it but this motherfucker doesn't get it."

"I get it," Boogie said. "It's just stupid."

"It's not stupid. It's smart," Johnny said, tapping the side of his head. "I wanna call it the New York Giants."

Everyone in the room laughed. Johnny tried to calm us down.

"Listen! Listen, you motherfuckers." He waved his hands around. "This is the thing: when people see 'Appearing tonight: the New York fucking Giants' on a flier, they're going to come to the goddamn show."

"They're going to come to the show expecting to see the fucking football team, dumbass," Boogie shouted. They'd obviously gone over this more times than Boogie wanted.

"Wouldn't that get you in trouble with the real New York Giants?" I asked.

"It don't matter. We'll have so many fucking fans by then we'll change it. We're just using it to get people to the goddamn shows."

"That's pretty smart," Alex said.

"See!" Johnny shouted, turning to Boogie. "He gets it. This motherfucker gets it."

"We ain't calling this band the New York Giants," Boogie said, covering his eyes with one hand. "Man, I can't take this shit."

We all laughed, even Johnny. With all the joking I felt like I could bring up the safe again.

"So that safe isn't here, man?"

"Nah," Boogie said. He sensed something. "Why? What's up?"

"We need to get it back."

"What the fuck for?" Boogie said. He looked at me. We were eye to eye even though he was sitting down.

"The owner wants it back."

"Is that right, Danny?" Boogie asked.

"Well, you see," Danny mumbled. "The guy we took it from sorta figured it out. And—"

"Now we had a deal, Danny," Boogie said, standing up. "You promised me five grand for hiding this motherfucker and getting it open. Who's gonna pay me my money?"

Danny stuttered and crossed his arms over his chest. He tried to talk.

"No, no, Boogie. See, I told him that we were gonna have to talk to you and work something out."

"Because I'm not going back to jail," Boogie said.

Finally, I thought, someone in this group with a brain. It felt like things were going my way. Thanks, Boogie.

"Exactly. Nobody wants to go to jail," I said. "The best thing is to just give it back and forget the whole mess."

"No." Boogie turned on me. "That's my Moog money."

"What the fuck is Moog money?" Alex asked.

"You know, a Moog. One of them fancy little keyboards. We need money to buy one."

"Yeah," said Johnny. "Stevie Wonder has one. So does Parliament. That shit costs over a grand. Plus, we need new drums."

My stomach flopped onto the dirty kitchen floor.

"The person that safe belongs to is not someone we really want to fuck with," I said.

"Some church motherfucker? That don't scare us," said Boogie.

"So you're gonna take on Backwoods Billy and the Holy Ghosts?" I asked.

Boogie and Johnny looked at each other with wide eyes. This was new information to them and the effect registered all over their faces.

"You took the safe from them motorcycle nuts?" Boogie said, stepping toward Danny. "You told me you got it from some church group."

"Well, I, uh . . ." Danny mumbled.

The way he shriveled reminded me of the time I was a kid and my mom caught me stealing a candy bar at Woolworth's and made me return it and apologize.

"That's sorta what I meant."

Boogie sat back down and rubbed his eyes. He wouldn't back down now.

"Fuck it. He don't know I'm involved." He pulled a snub-nosed pistol out of the back of his pants and slammed it on the table. "And if any of you motherfuckers tell him, it's your ass."

He jabbed a thick finger at me, Alex and Danny.

"We don't even know what's in the safe, Boogie," Alex said. I felt proud of him for finally saying something. "Might be nothing."

"There's got to be serious cash in there. That's a big safe. The kind where you put something you don't want no mother-fucker getting."

"How much do we have to pay you to get the safe back?" I asked.

Boogie stared at the floor. The room went quiet. After a few seconds he groaned loudly. "Fine. Tell ya what. You bring me two grand and I'll give it back to you untouched. Other-wise, I'm gonna drill that motherfucker."

Johnny's head nodded up and down behind me.

"We'll give you a thousand," I said.

"Two."

"You're crazy."

"Well, that's the gamble you're gonna have to take, white boy," Boogie said. "You can pay me two thousand for the safe or you can go back to Backwoods Billy and tell that fucking psycho you can't return what you stole from him, hand him a thousand bucks and pray to fucking God that's more cash than he had in there and he's willing to let this shit go instead of running over your head with a motorcycle."

I looked at Alex to see what he thought and he shook his head with a disgusted look on his face. Danny shrugged.

"All right," I said to Boogie. "Just don't touch that safe."

"No problem." He grinned.

No one spoke as we drove back to town. I looked over at Danny as we crossed Hanover Street Bridge. He created this mess but I was the one who Backwoods Billy was going to kill. He sat slouched in the seat next to me, shirt-sleeves rolled up, arm dangling out the window. I wanted to open his door and boot him, send him sailing into the Patapsco River.

Alex was quiet in the backseat. We were all scheming of ways to come up with two thousand dollars. There was no legal way to get that much money as quickly as we needed it. Not for guys like us. It would have to be something bad, something on a bigger scale than any of us were used to pulling off. Robbing Zeppelin was sounding better and better. Danny turned to Alex.

"Do you still talk to that Angie girl you used to sneak around with?" he asked.

Angie was an ugly girl. Dumpy with big, weird-shaped teeth and tiny eyes set too far apart on her face. A few years earlier Angie had won ten thousand dollars on *Let's Make a Deal*. Alex hooked up with her, convinced her to buy him a bunch of shit and then bailed once he'd cleaned her out. She never made the connection between the money drying up and Alex leaving and she still loved him madly. I dreaded running into her with Alex.

"Naw. I haven't talked to her in a long time. Why?"

"Isn't she a bank teller?"

"Yeah," Alex said. "Downtown."

"We're not robbing a fucking bank," I said, shaking my head.

"Maybe she'd be into it? We could cut her in for the ten grand Alex took from the poor girl," Danny joked. Alex laughed. "No, seriously. Do you think she'd help us?"

"No way," Alex said. "She's a nerdy chick, man. She ain't helping us rob a bank."

"What if we rob one anyway, you know, without her help?"

"I'm not robbing a bank," I said. "That's serious shit. People get shot doing that."

"And this town is so fucking small everyone working there would know us," Alex added.

"Not if we got some really cool masks."

"Forget it!" Alex and I yelled at the same time.

The Doors came on the radio. "Roadhouse Blues." I always liked the Doors. They never got caught up in the hippie bullshit. They did their own thing. They didn't play Woodstock or Monterey or any of that crap. They drank whiskey and wore black leather and Jim Morrison yelled at the crowd and pulled out his dick. You either loved or hated the Doors. I loved them.

I thought about a few quick ways to make the money to pay Boogie but none of them really worked out. Alex and Danny rambled about robbing banks or stealing cars. I knew the Zeppelin heist was our best chance. We'd just have to hold off Backwoods Billy until Zeppelin hit New York City that weekend.

On the radio, Morrison sang, "The future's uncertain and the end is always near."

THIRTEEN

the worst blow job in the world

keith stumbled ACROSS THE CARNIVAL GROUNDS, SWEATY AND SHIRTLESS AND LOADED OUT OF HIS MIND ON BLACK BEAUTIES AND BEER. THE BEER MADE KEITH CLUMSY BUT THE SPEED MADE HIM MOVE EVERYWHERE AS QUICKLY AS POSSIBLE. THE COMBINATION WAS HILARIOUS. I LEANED AGAINST MY CAR WITH ALEX AND FRENCHY AND WATCHED KEITH HURL TOWARD US WITH UTTER FUCKING ABANDON. HE MOVED AS FAST AS HE COULD IN A ZIGZAG. HIS ARMS FLAILED AS HE PLOWED THROUGH THE CROWD AND STAGGERED OVER THE UNEVEN GRASS.

We'd spent most of the day sitting at Keith's kitchen table drinking beer and plotting. We needed a tight plan if we still planned to rob Zeppelin. Every time one of us came up with a workable plan, someone else found a hole in it. By the time we came up with something we could all agree on, we were drunk.

We decided to hit the annual carnival on the Inner Harbor to celebrate. Every summer the city put together a carnival in honor of the city's goodwill and every year it turned into a drunken riot. The families cleared out by sunset when the festival turned into a circus of drugged-up kids and drunken criminals. There were fistfights and stabbings and wasted kids puking everywhere, more from the beer and drugs than the rides. It was the highlight of our summer.

First, we needed to hit the beer tent. The bartenders didn't take cash, only colored tickets sold at a table manned by an off-duty cop who checked IDs. We worked around this every year by stopping at the party supply store and buying rolls of tickets in every color and smuggling them into the tent.

We sent Keith to scope out which tickets they were using and he'd just returned. The speed made him talk in a jumble of words even before he got close enough for us to hear what he said.

"... then they told me I had to go I had to leave you know get out but I wasn't gonna until I saw the tickets but it was too dark to tell and a woman spilled her beer down my back but I didn't care so I went to the—"

"Keith!" Alex interrupted. "What color are the tickets?"

"Red. I think they're red. Hard to tell. I need some water or something my mouth is dry . . ."

Keith talked to Frenchy, who ignored him. Alex leaned into the trunk and rummaged through a shopping bag filled with rolls of tickets. When he found the red tickets we each pulled off a long strip and stuffed it into our pockets.

The beer tent barely covered the crowd under it and no one noticed when we ducked under the ropes in the back. We decided Alex looked the oldest and he shoved off through the crowd with a fistful of tickets to buy the first round of beers.

Sara showed up to hang out with Frenchy. They stood to the side talking. Now and then I caught her glaring at me, still mad about the incident with her purse. The speed kicked in hard and Keith babbled about everything from UFOs to his uncle's Mustang then back to UFOs and into a rant about how much he hated *Soul Train*. Alex returned with the beers.

"There are nothing but old women in here," he griped between sips of beer.

I couldn't see much over the wall of bodies but I knew he was right. The women in the beer tent looked like sad single mothers and forty-year-olds on a girls night out. Most of the girls our age hung out in the carnival, not the beer tent.

I turned to watch the neon-lit crowds moving around the dirt path that wound through the rides and games. Kids surrounded the bumper cars and a dinky roller coaster or tried to win prizes at any of the rigged games. Santana pumped through the speakers, mixing with the noise from the crowd. One laugh cut through it all.

"Emily!" I yelled toward her. She stood eating a foot-long corndog covered in ketchup.

"Oh my God!" She giggled as she walked over. "Great! And here I am eating a big-ass corndog."

"Who are you here with?"

"Tina and my friend Brandy."

"Tina's here?" Alex asked. "Where's she at?"

"Over there buying a funnel cake."

Alex drained the rest of the beer then ducked under the rope and walked off into the crowd. Emily licked ketchup off her fingers.

"I don't know if Tina wants to see him after everything that went down," she said.

"It'll be fine. No girl can stay mad at Alex."

"I don't know. He just got out of County! Tina is pretty tough."

"We'll see." I smiled.

The carnival crowd parted and Alex walked toward us laughing loudly, his arm around Tina. I never knew how he did it. Brandy walked alongside them. She was chubby but not quite fat. The bright yellow button-up shirt she wore fought to keep from bursting open around her tits, and her blond ponytail swung as she hurried to keep up with Alex and Tina.

"Come on," Alex told the girls. "I'll buy you a beer."

Soon we were all drunk and clustered in the corner of the tent talking. Tina tried to convince us that Elton John had talent, which caused me and Keith to groan. Alex claimed that white music died in the sixties and black music was the only thing worth buying. Frenchy kept bringing up the Kinks.

"Have you seen *Live and Let Die*?" Emily asked everyone. "James Bond is so fucking sexy."

"I always hated those movies," I said.

"How can you hate James Bond?"

"It's corny."

"It's not corny!"

"Criminals aren't like that. They don't sit around plotting big scams."

"They're criminal masterminds! That's how their minds work."

"There are no criminal masterminds. Trust me. Criminals just make shit up as they go along."

"Just like you're doing now." She laughed, leaning in to kiss me.

I overheard Keith chatting up Brandy. The beer he had drunk mellowed out the speed a little but he still rambled nervously.

"If you told me you gave the worst blow job in the world, I would say prove it."

"Oh really?" Brandy laughed and rolled her eyes.

"That's all I'm saying," Keith said, shrugging. He wobbled a bit. I nudged him in the ribs.

"Keith, man. What the fuck are you doing?"

"No. No. It's cool. We're just talking. It's cool."

Brandy looked at me and giggled. I couldn't believe she actually found Keith amusing.

Emily whispered something to me but I couldn't hear her. The noise on the other side of the tent suddenly grew louder.

Voices shouted back and forth. The crowd surged toward us. Someone stumbled into me, knocking the beer out of my hand. Something was wrong. Me and Alex traded worried looks and he pushed off through the crowd. Seconds later he broke through the wall of bodies.

"We gotta get the fuck out of here," he said, wide-eyed. "Right now. Let's fucking go."

"What going on?" Emily asked.

"We gotta go."

Clusters of people dropped their beers and scurried away. They shoved past us, ducking under the rope and hurrying away from the beer tent. Frenchy slipped through the crowd with his arm around Sara.

"What the fuck is happening?" he asked Alex.

Spend enough time around violence and bullshit and you develop a sense for it. You can smell a fight before it happens, while it's still just two guys trading hard looks from across a room. Having had the crap kicked out of me more than once before, my sense for trouble felt damn sharp. Something was going down on the other side of the tent and I didn't want any part of it.

"What the fuck are you gonna do about it, pretty boy?" someone shouted.

"Let's go. Come on. Let's just leave," a woman's voice pleaded.

"Hit that motherfucker!" another voice yelled.

"Do it, man! Do it!"

A fat man with a beard waddled past me shaking his head.

"It's those damn motorcycle riders," he said. "They're drunk and looking for trouble again."

I dropped my beer and bolted from the tent, pulling Emily along behind me. All of us moved in a group through the crowd and around the merry-go-round. No one wanted to look back. Terror crept up my spine and I finally glanced behind us. On the other side of the crowd a long, tattooed finger pointed right at me. The skull ring glistened in the neon lights.

"Shit! Shit!" I hissed under my breath. "He saw me."

Emily couldn't take any more.

"Tell me what is going on. Right now."

"You know the Holy Ghosts motorcycle gang?"

"Yeah."

"They don't like me very much."

"Patrick! What did you do? Shit. Goddamn it."

Backwoods Billy, Rabbit and a gang of dingy Holy Ghosts barged through the crowd and closed in on us. We ducked behind the concession stand then snaked between two tents and came out the other side behind the Tilt-a-Whirl. I led the way, hooking around a few carnival games and the fun house. Keith stumbled over a mess of cables and nearly knocked Alex to the ground. Frenchy looked worried.

We hurried through a path around the bumper cars and I felt like we had lost Backwoods Billy. I finally looked back. A pair of Holy Ghosts in leather jackets and bandannas walked through the crowd but they didn't seem to be after us. I turned back around just as Backwoods Billy and Rabbit rounded the corner up ahead and moved toward us. We were surrounded.

"Come on. We'll ride the Ferris wheel," Alex told everyone. "They won't see us."

"No fucking way," I said. "I'm not going on that thing."

"He's scared of heights," Frenchy told Sara.

"What a sissy," she sneered.

"Come on. We're getting on," Emily ordered me.

She pulled me up the metal steps to the bright green Ferris wheel. We cut the line of kids and began piling into cars. Me and Emily were last and I caught a glimpse of Backwoods Billy passing in the crowd just as a carny with thick arms locked the safety bar across us. The wheel jerked into motion and we rose above the crowd. I closed my eyes.

"Tell me what's going on. Can you see them?" I asked Emily.

"I think we're okay. It looks like they're leaving."

I exhaled the breath I had been holding since the beer tent and lay my head on the back of the metal seat. She leaned into me and squeezed my hand. I really fucking hated heights. The night air felt cooler as we climbed and I clenched my eyes tighter. Someone above us screamed and I heard metal rattling.

"What's that sound?" I panicked.

"Just Keith being an asshole. He's rocking the car and making Brandy scream."

Emily leaned forward, causing our car to tip.

"Hey! Hey! Cut it out!" I yelled.

"Sorry! Just trying to see where they went. I think they're gone."

The sound of the carnival quieted as we rounded the peak of the Ferris wheel. We were high enough to see the lights of the city. The skyline probably looked beautiful but I couldn't open my eyes.

We started our climb back toward the top and Emily shifted in her seat nervously. She leaned forward, tipping the car again, and I held my breath and clung to the metal safety bar.

"Oh my God," she whispered.

"What? What is it?"

"I think we're in trouble," she said.

"Why? What's happening?"

"Take a look."

I opened my eyes slowly. The entire city spread out in the distance, dotted with glowing orange lights. It did look beautiful. I tipped my head and glanced down. A sea of denim and leather and greasy hair surrounded the Ferris wheel. A few of the Holy Ghosts shoved people passing through the crowd. Someone threw a wild punch. The rest of the faces all pointed up toward us. One face with a long red beard and a tattooed neck stared straight at me.

Backwoods Billy smiled and waved.

The Ferris wheel slowed down and stopped. At the bottom, the operator opened the gate to let Alex and Tina out. Keith and Brandy were next. Then Frenchy and Sara. Me and Emily came around last. I stared at the floor of the car. My stomach flip-flopped.

"You feelin' all right, boy?" the carny asked, laying a large black hand on my shoulder as he helped me out of the Ferris wheel car. "You ain't gonna puke, are you?"

I shook my head and he stepped aside to let us out.

Backwoods Billy waited at the bottom of the stairs. He threw his arm around my shoulders as I came down the steps. His beard grated against the side of my face.

"'They that hate me without a cause are more than the hairs of my head,'" he hissed, spitting whiskey breath into my face as he talked. I pulled away from him and he yanked on my hair.

"Having a good fucking time, boy?"

He tugged harder on my hair, pulling my ear down to his shoulder.

"Where's my safe, you little asshole?"

Behind him, a biker with black hair and pockmarked skin leered at Tina.

"Come on, girl. I'll win you one of them pink elephants. Then we can go behind one of them tents out back."

He lunged at her and she darted behind Alex.

"Leave me alone, you fucking dirtbag," she shrieked.

I stared at Alex. He gave me a look that said he didn't know what to do either. Billy caught me looking.

"These friends of yours?" he asked, jerking a thumb over his shoulder. "You better tell me where that safe is before my boys tear 'em apart."

He poked a tattooed hand into my chest and twisted my hair as he spoke.

"'Destruction cometh; and they shall seek peace, and there shall be none.'"

"Is that another quote from the Good Book?"

"You better fucking believe it." He grinned, showing off a gold-capped tooth.

The carny operating the Ferris wheel yelled from the top of the steps, "Hey! What's going on down there?"

"Everything's fine, bud." Billy grinned up at him.

"Well, move along," the carny said. "You can't stand there."

Billy ignored him and turned back to me.

"Where's the safe, kid?"

"I don't have it. I swear I don't have it."

"Who has it?"

"A guy we know. He won't give it back until I pay him."

He looked genuinely shocked.

"Some asshole is holding my fucking safe ransom? *My fucking safe!*"

He screamed into my face. I prayed someone in the crowd would step in but no one did. Not a single head turned in the passing crowd or the Ferris wheel line. No one wanted to get involved. Most of the crowd spotted the pack of sweaty greasers in Holy Ghosts vests and then walked the other way.

"Listen, boy. You're gonna show me where this motherfucker lives and we're gonna get that safe if I have to cut his fucking throat."

He slid a finger across my neck.

"I'll get it. I swear. I just need a little time."

Behind us, a pair of scraggly Holy Ghosts terrorized Alex and Keith. They looked like lesser members of the gang. Younger guys trying to make a name. A chubby biker with a bald head joined his buddy with the bad skin.

"Let us borrow your dates, fellas. We'll have 'em back by morning, I swear. They'll have a real good time."

"Yeah. We'll be on our best behavior," the bald guy said, holding a leather-gloved hand over his heart.

The carny reappeared at the top of the stairs.

"I told you once already," he said, pointing at Backwoods Billy. "Move the fuck along."

"Mind your own fucking business," Billy snarled.

"This *is* my business, you honky asshole. Now get the fuck out of here."

"Shut your fucking mouth, carny," Billy snapped.

The carny moved fast for a guy with the build of someone who sits at a Ferris wheel all day.

"Get your ass out of here!" he shouted as his steel-toed boots thundered down the metal steps.

A long arm in a black leather jacket shot up behind him and swung down. The bottle exploded over the carny's head. He bent at the waist and covered his head with his hands.

Then all hell broke loose.

Carnival workers appeared from everywhere. They leapt over counters and charged out of trailers. Every hand held a weapon. Baseball bats. Mop handles. Screwdrivers. The crowd swirled as carnies and Holy Ghosts squared off. As hard as the carnies beat them, the Holy Ghosts kept getting back up.

Alex only needed one chance. He latched on to two fistfuls of hair hanging in the biker's pockmarked face, pulled down and shot his knee up. The biker's nose crunched. Alex swung him by the hair, twisting him around until Keith kicked the biker's legs out, knocking him to his knees. The skinny black kid who operated the Tilt-a-Whirl stepped forward and swung a tennis racket like he was returning a rocket of a volley. The strings raked across the biker's face and the wooden frame shattered over his skull.

A Holy Ghost stomped a thick boot into the face of a limp

body on the ground. A carny split a broom handle over his head but the biker barely flinched. He spun, grabbed the carny by the hair and punched him in the throat, sending him gasping to the ground.

Backwoods Billy never let go of me. He bulldozed backward, using me as a battering ram to break through the chaos. The first punch slammed into my eye. He jerked my arm toward him as he threw it, doubling the impact. His fist seemed to fill my entire eye socket. A Holy Ghost slipped behind me and bear-hugged me, pinning my arms at my sides. He lifted me off the ground.

"You're coming with us," he grunted.

I kicked out at both of them but without a foot on the ground for leverage, the blows bounced off. I buried my chin into my chest and wagged my head from side to side as fists hammered into the top of my head. One lucky shot slipped low on my forehead, tearing open the skin. Blood poured into my eyes. An uppercut crammed my lower lip into my teeth. I tasted blood.

The Holy Ghost behind me lifted my body off the ground, turned it sideways and slammed me onto the ground. I should have stayed down but didn't. A foot crashed into my lower back as I tried to stand. My body flattened into the gravel. Kicks and punches landed from everywhere. I didn't even think about getting up. I curled in a ball and covered my head. Hands pried my arms away from my head to make holes for fists to slip through. My mouth filled with gravel and dust.

"All right! All right!" Backwoods Billy yelled. He stepped forward and waved away the circle of jackals beating on me.

"Lemme talk to him," he said.

Through the eye that wasn't swollen closed I saw Backwoods Billy bend and lift me up by my shirt collar. I stumbled and crashed onto my back. His grip slipped and I scrambled backward up the steps.

The Ferris wheel worker rose behind him. Blood and broken glass streamed down his head. He fumbled in his pocket then swung a heavy metal wrench high over his head. I had every chance to say something. Every chance to warn Backwoods Billy before the wrench split his skull.

I didn't say a fucking thing.

The wrench ricocheted off the back of Backwoods Billy's head. Blood streamed down his face. He howled with pain and flung both arms over his head. The carny pried loose one arm and dragged Backwoods Billy backward into the crowd by his wrist. His motorcycle boots kicked in the dust as he tried to stand. A carny in a white apron leapt forward and cracked a pool cue across Backwoods Billy's ribs.

"I'll find you motherfucker! I want my fucking safe!" he screamed at me.

I stumbled forward, dodging swinging fists and sidestepping someone lying facedown in a pool of blood. Alex and Frenchy stood in a clearing on the other side of the swirling fighters. Behind them, a wall of police officers prepared to swarm into the brawl.

"Where are the girls?"

"They bailed the second this shit started," Alex told me.

"Where's Keith?" I said, scanning the area for him. Alex's head spun around.

"Shit," he hissed. "He must have run too."

Police radios crackled around us. Suddenly the Baltimore Police raised their batons and streamed into the crowd.

"Let's go," Frenchy shouted.

He lifted a red tent skirt and we scurried underneath. Boxes of toy prizes and giant stuffed bears cluttered the dark tent. We plowed through the tent flaps on the other side and sprinted across the fairgrounds toward my car, lost in the orange lights in the distance.

FOURTEEN
piss test

i couldn't PISS.

"That's okay, honey," the chubby nurse said to me from the other side of the bathroom door in my hospital room. "You just need to relax. We'll try again later."

Frenchy insisted on bringing me to the hospital. The doctor figured the beating left me with a minor concussion, maybe a few cracked ribs. Otherwise I was all right. He made me stay the night and told me if they didn't find any blood in my piss I might be able to go home early. Only I couldn't piss.

My folks came by a few hours later. I told them I'd been beaten up and robbed for my watch. Not a total lie. Mom rushed into the room and hugged me, which made my vision go blurry. My dad stood at the end of the bed and told me I shouldn't have been downtown anyway. Then he babbled about the hospital's outdated fire alarm system. When I'd heard enough, I told them to leave so I could get some sleep. In the morning the nurse entered my room.

"You have a visitor."

Emily poked her head around the corner.

"How are ya feeling, champ?"

"I'm all right, Emily. How are you?"

She pulled a chair over to the edge of the bed and sat down, crossing her long legs and kicking one sandaled foot back and forth. Her cutoff jeans and white tank top clung to her.

"How did you know I was here?" I asked.

"Tina told me."

Alex must have told her. Emily sighed loudly.

"You heard about Keith?" she asked.

"What about him?"

"He's in jail."

I sat up in bed. A bolt of pain shot through my ribs.

"What for?"

"I don't know," Emily said. "They arrested him and a bunch of those motorcycle nuts."

"Shit," I groaned.

I pictured Keith in a tiny holding cell, surrounded by Holy Ghosts. I had to get in touch with Alex and find a way to bail Keith out.

"Patrick!" Emily shouted. "Are you listening to me?"

"Yeah. Sorry. I'm listening."

"So?"

"So what?"

"So what happened? What was all that about?"

"Just a misunderstanding," I lied. "Something to do with Alex's uncle Danny."

She didn't believe me but let it go.

"When are you getting out of here?" she asked.

"As soon as he gives me a pee-pee sample," the nurse said, walking into the room holding up a clear plastic cup. I sunk into the bed. Emily giggled.

"Aww. I'll let you . . . uh . . . take care of things. But we should hang out when you get out of here. I'm worried about you."

When she was gone I padded barefoot into the bathroom.

"Maybe that visit from your girlfriend relaxed you," the nurse said from outside the bathroom door. I stood in front of the toilet with my hospital gown open and thought about getting out of there, settling things with Backwoods Billy and spending time with Emily.

The nurse was right. I pissed long and hard until I was nearly out of breath.

"You have another visitor, honey. I'll come back."

I snapped the lid on the cup of piss. When I opened the door a man in a suit stood in the middle of the room. He looked at me and my cup of piss.

"Hey, Patrick. It's Patrick, right? How are you feeling?"

"I'm okay."

I left the piss on the counter and climbed back into bed.

"You a doctor or something?" I asked.

"You don't know who I am?"

He didn't give me a chance to answer.

"Of course you don't. You're just a fucking teenager," he said, talking to himself more than me. "I'm Simon Cooper. District Attorney."

I stiffened in bed. He started to shake my hand but his eyes caught the cup of piss on the counter. He pulled his hand back.

"You know what a district attorney is?"

"Yeah."

"Really?" He smiled. "Did I put one of your friends in jail or something? Maybe your father? You don't hold some grudge against me, do you? Not gonna try to stab me?"

"Depends. What do you want?"

He laughed and scratched his head. His messy hair stuck up in dark tufts above glasses that looked too tight for his box-shaped head. The gray flecks at his temples matched his wrinkled shirt.

"So, what happened last night down at the harbor?"

"Some guys tried to rob me. No big deal."

"Really? Did the police catch them?"

"Nah. Could have been anyone."

"Wasn't any of the Holy Ghosts, was it?" he smirked.

I shrugged. He paced the room and stared at the floor.

"So some guys beat you up and tried to rob you right in the middle of the carnival? Worked you over pretty bad, right? I mean, here you are."

He chuckled. I didn't like where this was going.

"What do you want?"

"Listen," he said. "I'm not after you. Not at all. It's just that a cop friend working the carnival last night thought maybe he overheard you say something to my friend, our friend Back-woods Billy. Something that could really help me out and then maybe help you out in the future too."

He stood at the foot of the bed waiting for me to say some-thing. I didn't say anything.

"Something about a safe, maybe? Maybe I'm wrong. Am I wrong? Is that not what you said?"

I didn't say a word. His fingers tapped nervously on the edge of the bed.

"I understand, Patrick. I really do. But see, there's a chance, just a small chance, really, that there's something in that safe that is, uh, very valuable to me. More valuable than you might even realize. Do you know what I'm talking about?"

I didn't. We hadn't opened the safe. Now I wanted to know what was in there.

"Can I smoke in here?" he asked, holding a cigarette in his fingers. He leaned to look out the door into the hallway. "No. No. I probably can't."

His fidgeting grew worse and his fingers fumbled around in his pants pockets. He started to sweat.

"Am I under arrest or something?" I said.

"No! No." He stuck out his arms and gave me a face like I had to be kidding. Like we were old friends and how dare I suggest such a thing. "Not at all. Nothing like that. I'm just trying to track something down and thought maybe you had it."

"What is it?"

"Well, see," he smiled, "I can't really say too much. Nothing against you. It's just something between me and Billy that I've been trying to get back from him. This would just make it easier, you know, to get it from you."

I nodded.

"Kind of hard to tell you if I have it or not if I don't know what it is we're talking about."

"Just look around," he said. "I'll leave my card for you. If you come across it, give me a call. No questions asked."

He placed his card on the counter next to a water pitcher and some medicine the doctor left me. He lifted a bottle of pills.

"Are these Percocet? Wow. Ever taken them? These are . . . wow. You'll have a good time with these."

He shook the bottle at me and smiled.

"He really gave you a lot. Mind if I take a few?"

Outside in the hallway I heard the nurse talking loudly.

"Boys. Boys! You can't go in there. Stop right there!"

Alex and Frenchy charged into the room, doubled over laughing. The front of Alex's T-shirt said, "Delcon Industrial Strength Weed Killer." He froze when he saw Simon and stared at him suspiciously.

"Who the fuck is this guy?"

"Just a friend, gentlemen. He's all yours. I was just leaving," Cooper said, moving toward the door. He stopped in front of Alex. "Actually, are you guys in the gardening or landscaping business? I noticed your shirt and thought . . ."

Alex could sniff out authority and he hated it. He stared at Cooper like he had just asked if Alex ate shit sandwiches.

"No," Alex snarled, lighting up a cigarette. "It says 'weed' on it. It's funny."

"Oh, yes. Of course. Really funny. Okay, guys. Um, take it easy."

Alex pointed at Cooper.

"Seriously, Patrick. Who the fuck is this guy?"

After Cooper left, I told Alex and Frenchy about how he asked about the safe.

"So, what's in it?" I wondered out loud.

"I think there's a ton of cash in there," Alex said.

"Has gotta be," I agreed.

"Or maybe Backwoods Billy stole something from this Cooper guy and it's in the safe and he hasn't been able to get it back," Frenchy said.

"Nah. He's a DA. If he thought Billy stole something from him he'd just have Billy arrested."

"Whatever's in that safe, they both want it," I said. "They both want it really fucking bad."

This changed everything. Alex picked up the phone.

"Hey, Boogie. It's Alex. New plan. You know that safe? Open that fucker up."

Alex covered the phone with one hand and looked at me.

"He says Danny already called and told him to open it. They've almost got it."

Frenchy sighed and sat down on the counter, knocking my bottle of pills to the ground. He bent to pick it up.

"Holy shit! Percocet? Mind if I take a few?"

FIFTEEN
snowbirds

the telephone RANG THE NEXT DAY. I CRINGED IN PAIN AS I HOBBLED TOWARD THE KITCHEN TO ANSWER IT. MY RIBS STILL HURT. I'D BEEN LET OUT OF THE HOSPITAL EARLIER WITH MY PERCOCET AND A WARNING TO TAKE IT EASY. I KNEW IT WAS ALEX BEFORE I ANSWERED.

"Boogie called."

"He got the safe open?" I asked.

"Just about. He wants us to come by."

"Did he say what was in it? Could he see?"

"Wouldn't tell me. Just said that he wanted to meet at his shop in an hour."

"He wouldn't tell you?"

"Nope. He kept laughing and told me that we needed to come see for ourselves."

He paused.

"Think there's enough in there to bail Keith out?"

"Let's hope. Where's the shop?"

Boogie's shop took up the back room of a tire garage on the east side of town. He stood in front of the open garage door as me and Alex pulled up at the address. His Funkadelic T-shirt hung loosely and he tugged at his blossoming Afro with a black pick. A huge grin spread across his face and he sang loudly as me and Alex walked up: "Spread your tiny wings and fly away, and take the snow back with you where it came from on that day."

"What the hell are you singing?" Alex asked.

Boogie smiled and motioned for us to follow him through the garage. Stacks of tires covered the concrete floor. A muscular black guy pounded on a steel rim at a tool bench. In the back, an air gun pumped loudly. Three soda machines, probably left over from Boogie's business, sat along the wall.

At a closed office door in the back corner Boogie turned to face me and Alex. He flung open the office door and sang loudly as he ducked through the doorway: "The one I love is forever untrue and if I could you know I'd fly away with you."

Me and Alex both laughed. I didn't know what the hell Boogie was singing but he seemed to be in a good mood. I took that as a good sign. Maybe things were going to work out. I limped through the store behind them trying not to fall over anything.

Johnny Paycheck and a few other guys sat in mismatched chairs and played dominoes on an old card table. R&B blasted from a tiny radio. A double-barrel shotgun leaned against the wall and a pistol lay on the counter. Paycheck looked up when he heard Boogie singing.

"Was that you singing?" Paycheck asked.

Boogie nodded.

"You know, that's just fucked up." Paycheck laughed. "You're one sick motherfucker."

Boogie's deep laugh rumbled from his chest.

A tall gray safe sat in the corner. It was enormous, and for a second I was amazed that Danny and Alex had even been able to carry it. The thick steel looked impenetrable. An older black man with thick glasses and a bald head leaned over the safe. He stared into a small scope stuck in a hole drilled in the door. He slowly turned the combination dial with one hand.

"Is that the safe?" I asked.

"You mean you never saw this shit?" Boogie grinned. "They tried to kill you for stealing this and you never even saw it?"

Everyone in the room laughed. Everyone but me and Alex.

"Goddamn, son." Paycheck grinned.

"Danny really fucked him over, right?" Boogie asked with a smile.

"Hell yeah," Paycheck said, grinning.

"Any idea what's inside?" Alex asked, crossing his arms over his chest.

"Oh, we got an idea." Boogie grinned. "We took a look around with the scope."

"Just about got it," the old guy said.

The dial clicked loudly and the old guy stepped out of the way. Boogie stood in front of the safe. He slammed down on the handle and flung open the heavy door with a magician's flourish.

"Ta-da!" he yelled.

Me and Alex both stepped forward. Neither one of us could believe it. The cold steel walls, the wide top shelf, all of it sat empty except for the bottom of the safe, which held two dusty reel-to-reel tapes: Jim Nabors's *Galveston* and Anne Murray's *Snowbird*.

Boogie started to sing. Johnny joined him.

"So, little snowbird, take me with you when you go to that land of gentle breezes where the peaceful waters flow."

They howled with laughter and Johnny pounded on the table with his fist.

"Jim fucking Nabors." Paycheck laughed hysterically. "That motherfucker played Gomer Pyle. Why you gonna buy an album by Gomer fucking Pyle?"

"Man, that's cold," one of the domino players said, shaking his head.

"We're so fucked," I mumbled to Alex. "Jesus Christ. He's gonna kill me."

"Nah," the safecracker said, trying to calm me down. "Just give the safe back to that biker asshole and walk the fuck away."

"How are we supposed to do that?" I pointed at the drilled hole in the front. "What about this? It's ruined now."

"Buy another safe just like this one."

"The combination would be different. I think he'd notice that."

"I can switch the locks," the old guy said, lighting a cigarette. "No problem."

Boogie picked at his hair.

"All right." I sighed loudly. "I guess we don't have a choice. Do that and we'll be back on Sunday."

"Don't forget," Boogie said. "Two grand. Plus the cost of the new safe. Otherwise I'll sink this motherfucker in the river."

"And if the Holy Ghosts sink me in the fucking river first," I huffed as I walked away, "I'll wait for you at the bottom."

Alex walked alongside me with his head down as we left the tire shop.

"You all right?" he asked.

"Yeah," I answered. "Why?"

"You seem pretty freaked out. I've never seen you like this."

"This was supposed to be so easy. Follow Zeppelin to the hotel. Take the money."

"Shit definitely went haywire," he said. He stopped on the sidewalk to light a cigarette.

"'Snowbird' by Anne Murray," I said.

"Is that what he was singing?"

Behind us, Boogie sang from the office.

"When I was young my heart was young then too, and anything that it would tell me, that's the thing that I would do."

"What a fucking asshole," Alex sneered.

SIXTEEN

book 'em, danno

keith looked BETTER IN THE BALTIMORE COUNTY JAIL THAN HE EVER DID ON THE OUTSIDE. HE WALKED INTO THE VISITORS' ROOM LOOKING RESTED, FED AND BATHED FOR THE FIRST TIME IN YEARS. NO FOOD STAINS ON HIS ORANGE JUMPSUIT. HE LEANED FORWARD, PLACED HIS HANDCUFFED WRISTS ON THE METAL TABLE AND TOLD ME AND ALEX HOW MUCH HE LOVED JAIL.

"Guess what I watched today, Alex? Remember that episode of *Hawaii Five-O* where the hippie kid asks that old dude for money and the old dude tries touching the kid's dick and the hippie kid punches him in the head and steals his wallet?"

"That's a fucking great one," Alex said. "It turns out the old guy had two hundred and fifty thousand dollars in a storage locker."

"Yeah. And that hippie chick ODs and they play all that weird trippy music."

"And that bartender gives them those licorice-flavored rolling papers?"

Keith sighed happily.

"Man. Licorice-flavored rolling papers. Can you imagine?"

"That's a good one."

"A classic, man. A classic. *Hawaii Five-O* is the best TV show ever."

The visitors' room at the county jail looked just like it did a few years ago when Alex made me come with him to visit Danny. The ocean blue concrete walls still held the corkboard covered with posters announcing the rules, such as NO TOUCH-ING and VISITORS UNDER THE INFLUENCE OF ALCOHOL OR DRUGS WILL BE EXPELLED. Guards stood against one wall observing the metal tables where prisoners sat with girlfriends and family. Two doors faced off on opposite walls. One door led back to the prison, the other door to the outside. I'd be leaving through one. Keith would not.

"So they're treating you all right in here?" I asked.

"Pretty much. It ain't bad, really. I watch TV all day and smoke. Hell, I'd be doing the same thing at home anyway."

A guard carrying a shotgun yawned as he walked past us. When he returned to the corner, Alex leaned forward.

"So what are they charging you with, anyway?" he asked.

"They think I'm one of the Holy Ghosts," Keith said with wide eyes.

Me and Alex found that hysterical: poor, dumb Keith a member of the most bloodthirsty pack of psychos in town.

"Fucking cops," Keith said softly. "That fight got crazy. Carnies and Holy Ghosts clubbing each other. Then the cops ran in and started busting up heads. I tried running but a cop coming the other way grabbed me."

Keith stubbed out his cigarette.

"They stuffed me in a paddy wagon. It was filled with dudes. Holy Ghosts on one side, carnies on the other. They were spitting on each other and going nuts. Kicking each

other across the aisle. This big-ass carny across from me kept staring at me. We turned a corner and he came at me. Landed on top of me and head-butted me in the eye."

He showed us the bruise on his temple.

"How much is your bail?" I asked.

"I don't know. They don't even know what they're charging me with. I heard something about felony assault or felony riot. One of the Holy Ghosts said something about us getting five years. Shit. Hopefully they'll figure out I ain't no Holy Ghost and let me out of here. I tell you one thing I am scared of, though."

He leaned across the table. His face grew tight with fear. He waited to talk until the guard walked to the other side of the room.

"They're gonna cut my hair, aren't they?"

"Why would they do that?"

"That's what they do! They give everybody a crew cut."

"That's the army, Keith."

"Naw. Happens in prison too."

"No, it doesn't," Alex said. "Look around the room. All these dudes have hair."

Alex kept talking but the words were lost in shouts from across the room. A tall inmate in a jumpsuit pounded his handcuffed fists on the metal table. Veins pulsated across his bald head. He kept screaming.

"You're a fucking dead man!"

He rocketed to his feet. The metal chair under him shot backward, slamming into the wall before clanging to the ground. Three guards struggled to restrain him. Every muscle in his body rippled with anger.

"You're dead! You're fucking dead!"

I didn't want to be whoever this guy was threatening. My eyes met his. Shit. I *was* the guy he was threatening.

"You don't know who you're fucking with!"

My stomach twisted in knots.

"Oh yeah," Keith said, calmly turning his head. "All the Holy Ghosts want to kill you. I heard Backwoods Billy's offering a reward for anybody who brings in you and that safe."

"How much is the reward?" Alex asked with a smile.

"Hopefully enough to bail me out," Keith joked.

I swallowed hard.

"By the way, Boogie opened the safe," Alex whispered to Keith. "Know what was in it?"

Keith shook his head.

"Two reel-to-reel tapes."

Keith shook his head.

"Where's the guitar?" he asked.

"Under the couch in Frenchy's basement," I answered.

"You guys still going to New York? You know, for that thing?" he asked.

"It's our only hope." I shrugged. "That money could get you out of here and buy that safe back from Boogie."

"Did you come up with a new plan yet? I don't think I'm gonna make it."

He held up his handcuffed wrists.

This was a serious problem. I hadn't even thought about it. We'd gone over every possible angle for this thing and devised an airtight plan. It needed to be perfectly timed using four people, not three. My head hurt and I rubbed my temples. Alex hadn't said a word but I knew what he was thinking.

"Shit. I guess we need to find a fourth person to make this work."

A guard stepped up behind Keith and kicked the back of his chair.

"Visiting hours are over, asshole."

We promised Keith we'd get him out of there as soon as we

could. He wished us luck and told us to look for licorice-flavored rolling papers in New York City.

As me and Alex pulled out of the parking lot I turned left and headed toward the one place I already knew Alex was going to suggest. He finally spoke up.

"Danny's?"

"Yeah." I sighed. "Damn it."

SEVENTEEN
la-z-boy

Danny wouldn't LOOK AT ME. NOT EVEN AFTER ME AND ALEX EXPLAINED THE PLAN AND HOW MUCH MONEY WE COULD MAKE IF WE PULLED IT OFF. HE STRETCHED OUT IN A LA-Z-BOY CHAIR IN HIS MOM'S BASEMENT AND STARED AT AN OLD WOODEN TV FLICKERING IN THE DARK WHILE WE TALKED. NOW AND THEN HE DUG HIS HAND INTO A BAG OF PIGGLY WIGGLY CHEESE PUFFS AND SHOVED THEM IN HIS MOUTH. POWDERED CHEESE CLUNG TO HIS BUSHY HANDLEBAR MUSTACHE AND SPRINKLED ON HIS BARE CHEST. HIS BEER BELLY DROOPED OVER THE WAISTBAND OF EMERALD GREEN SWEATPANTS.

"What do you think?" Alex asked.

Danny stubbed out his cigarette in an overflowing ashtray.

"Well, I don't know, boys. I'm not even supposed to leave the state since I'm on probation."

"Me neither." Alex shrugged. "We'll be there and back the same day. No one will even know we're gone."

"And I'll tell you what else is bugging me. Why Zeppelin? Shit, man. They're one of the best bands around."

He started singing. His head shook and he strummed an invisible guitar.

"'It's been a long time since I rock 'n' rolled. Dun duh. Dun duh dun duh.' I mean, damn, that's a great fucking tune, man."

Alex stopped me before I could talk.

"This has nothing to do with them. We just grab the money, pay off Boogie, get Keith out of jail and divide up the rest."

Danny thought for a few seconds, sipped from his beer and then sat back in the recliner.

"Nah. I think I'll sit this one out." Danny shrugged. "Good luck, Alex."

Alex shot me a panicked look. He didn't know what to say. I did.

"So, Danny, did Alex tell you that Boogie got the safe open?"

That got his attention. He lurched forward in the chair and tossed the cheese puffs on a TV tray cluttered with empty beer cans. He wiped his hands on his sweatpants, leaving a streak of orange cheese.

"Well, shit. No. No, he did not. When did this happen?"

"This morning. Want to know what was in it?"

"Hell yes, I do."

"Two old reel-to-reel tapes. That's it."

"You're shitting me!"

"Anne Murray and Jim Nabors."

He looked at Alex in disbelief. Alex nodded. Danny groaned then his head drooped. He rubbed his eyes then stared up at the ceiling. He was counting on that safe to be his big score and it wasn't. This was a broken man. He let out a long, agonized sigh, lit a cigarette and leaned forward.

"So you'll help us?" I asked.

"No. I still ain't gonna do it. I can't risk it. Some of us got responsibilities, Patrick. I can't be getting arrested. No sir. I'm getting my shit together."

Alex's Grandma Alice came down the stairs carrying a basket of dirty laundry.

"Hey, Grandma," Alex said.

"Hi, boys," she said.

She stopped and stared at Danny.

"Are those my sweatpants?" she yelled. "Goddamn it, Daniel! How many times have I told you not to wear my damn sweatpants! Look at 'em. You got cheese puffs all over 'em."

"Grandma! We're talking here. Go upstairs."

"You need to talk about getting a job, Daniel. This shit has gone on long enough. You need to get your ass out of this basement and get to work."

"I know! I'm working on it. Now give us a minute."

Grandma Alice trudged up the stairs muttering. When the basement door closed, Danny stood up and brushed the cheese puff crumbs off his chest.

"Well, boys," he said. "I'll tell ya what. I'm gonna help you out, but just this once."

EIGHTEEN

nobody's fault but mine

i couldn't STOP STARING AT THE LIP-GLOSSED MOUTH ON THE GIRL ACROSS FROM ME. SHE SAT SLUMPED OVER IN A CHAIR IN THE LOBBY OF THE DRAKE HOTEL WITH HER FACE BURIED UNDER ENORMOUS SUNGLASSES AND A FEATHER BOA. A WHITE MINISKIRT CREPT UP HER THIGHS. SHE SLEPT WITH HER HEAD TILTED STRAIGHT BACK, SNORING VIOLENTLY, WITH BRIGHT RED LIP GLOSS SMEARED AROUND HER MOUTH.

Frenchy was the first to say what we were all thinking.

"Keith would have loved this."

"He would have put something in that chick's mouth," I said.

"Probably his balls." Alex grinned.

A midafternoon party raged around the couch where I sat sandwiched between Frenchy and Alex. Drunken people filled the chairs and couches and crowded near the elevators waiting for any sign of Zeppelin. Most of the partiers were women who had spent all night, maybe even all weekend, trying to meet the band. Everyone seemed wasted or at least running on the fumes from last night's partying. The mood was ugly but the groupies weren't leaving. It was Sunday, Zeppelin's last gig at Madison Square Garden before the band headed back to London. It was the last chance for fans to party with Zeppelin and our last chance to snatch the money. No bank was open on Sunday so we had all day to find the money from last night's gig.

Alex looked around the lobby.

"I can't believe the women here."

His head swiveled backward.

"Oh my God! Look at her. Should I go talk to her?"

"We're not here to meet women, Alex," I reminded him.

"Fine," he huffed, slouching back into the couch.

A chauffer walked quickly across the lobby to the front desk. He wore a short-brimmed chauffeur's hat over dark hair slicked back in a ponytail that hung down over his collar. In one hand he carried a large guitar case.

The hotel clerk behind the desk looked worn down from the drunken carnival in the lobby. Over the past few days he'd dealt with the most fucked-up and deranged people in the city and his face showed it. He snapped at the chauffeur. "Is there something I can help you with?"

"Yeah. You can tell me where I can find Richard Cole. Those Led Zeppelin boys left this guitar in my limo and I need to give it to them."

"Sir, we've been instructed not to disturb Mr. Cole. Would you like to leave the guitar here with me?"

The chauffeur struggled to lift the guitar case up to the counter. He slammed it down on the wooden countertop and sent a white phone crashing to the floor. The guitar case clasps opened with loud snaps and the chauffeur lifted the lid.

"This is a nineteen fifty-eight Gibson Les Paul. One of only seventeen hundred in existence. It belongs to Mr. Jimmy Page.

You think I trust you or any of the mongrels in this lobby around this guitar?"

He pointed wildly around the room. The hotel clerk stared at the guitar while he fumbled to pick the phone up off the floor. "Well, sir, I uh . . ." he muttered.

A barefoot girl in skintight jeans and a half-shirt walked around the counter behind him. A bottle of wine dangled loosely in one hand. She opened an office door, peered inside, then walked away, leaving it open.

"Hey, man," she slurred to the clerk. "Where's the bathroom?"

"Down the hall," he pointed.

"You see what I'm talking about?" the chauffeur said. "That girl wouldn't have thought twice about walking right off with this thing. Then Zeppelin would have your ass and mine."

The chauffeur leaned forward and talked low.

"Now I ain't accusing you of anything, bud. I can just tell that you're understaffed and overworked here. This is a goddamn circus. You can't be expected to handle all this alone. Let me know where I can find Richard Cole and I'll be out of your way."

The clerk exhaled loudly and nodded. He flipped through a ledger on the desk.

"Mr. Cole is in room twenty-one-ten on the top floor."

"I appreciate it," the chauffeur said. He dragged the guitar case off the counter and walked toward the elevator. He stared straight at me and winked as he passed.

"I can't believe Danny pulled that off," Frenchy said.

"Of course he did." Alex grinned. "He's a Carter. We're born bullshitters."

"Where'd he get the chauffeur outfit?" Frenchy asked.

"I borrowed it from Carmine," I answered.

"He looks good."

Frenchy grabbed the guitar case at his feet. He'd insisted on bringing his beaten-up Fender Telecaster just in case Jimmy Page wanted to buy that too.

We slipped into the elevator with Danny. I didn't look at him. His pissing and moaning on the drive up here nearly broke me. When he wasn't complaining about the traffic or my car or the music, he talked endless shit about himself. I already swore to myself that he was sitting in the backseat on the way home.

Danny dropped the case holding the '58 Les Paul with a heavy thud as soon as the elevator doors closed.

"Take it easy!" Frency hissed. "That guitar is really rare."

"Then you carry this goddamn thing, Frenchy. Fucking guitar weighs a ton."

He tossed the chauffeur's cap on the ground and loosened his tie.

"Fuck. How much longer do I gotta wear this shit?"

"Not long. Just keep it together."

"Don't tell me to hold it together, Patrick."

I looked at Alex and rolled my eyes.

"I don't see why I have to be the one in a fucking costume," he whined.

"Because you're the oldest," I said.

I clipped an ID card to his pocket and handed him a walkie-talkie.

"Now remember to clear the hallways. We don't want any of these hippies around. Do whatever you have to do to get them off the floor."

"With fucking pleasure." He grinned.

The elevator doors opened on the twenty-first floor. A wave of pot smoke snaked into the elevator. People filled the hallways drinking beer and smoking among empty bottles and trash. As we stepped off the elevator a pair of shirtless girls ran past us giggling. We stopped at room 2110.

"All right, Frenchy," I said. "You know what to do."

Me and Alex stood at the other end of the hallway and tried to blend in with the rest of the madness. Frenchy smoothed his fake mustache, straightened his sunglasses, then knocked. No one answered. Frenchy looked over and shrugged. I signaled for him to knock again and he beat on the door.

A guy with pork-chop sideburns and thick glasses stopped in front of Danny. His frizzy hair blocked our view of Frenchy.

"Wow, man. Do you work here?"

"Yeah," Danny said.

He stepped forward into the kid's face.

"I need you to exit this floor immediately."

"I don't have to go anywhere."

Danny leaned in closer.

"You can go down the elevator or through a window. What's it gonna be?"

"You can't fucking do that—"

Danny shoved him before he stopped talking. The guy reeled backward, tangled his legs with two men sitting on the floor sniffing something off a mirror and crashed onto the ground. Everyone started arguing.

"Clear the floor, assholes," Danny yelled.

Frenchy stood in the hallway talking to Richard Cole. He looked taller than I remembered. He leaned in the doorway, rubbing a thick beard. His white shirt hung unbuttoned to the middle of his chest. Everything about his body language said he didn't want Frenchy bothering him. He crossed his arms while Frenchy talked. We couldn't hear what Frenchy said but before he finished Richard waved him off and started to close the door. Frenchy quickly opened the guitar case.

Richard glanced at the Les Paul just before he closed the

door. He looked impressed. Without taking his eyes off the guitar he signaled for Frenchy to stay put then shut his door.

"What the fuck is going on?" Alex asked me.

"I don't know." I was worried.

Frenchy looked over and shrugged. The door opened again and Richard stepped out. He pulled the door closed behind him and led Frenchy down to the end of the hallway. They stopped and Richard knocked softly then leaned forward and said something through the closed door. The door opened slowly and Richard led Frenchy inside.

"Okay. You know what to do."

"Sure do."

Alex pulled a thin piece of metal the size of a credit card out of his pocket and palmed it as we moved quickly to room 2110. Alex crouched behind me jimmying the door open. The metal card scraped again and again through the door frame but the lock wouldn't give.

"What the hell is going on?" I asked without looking back.

"I'm getting it. I'm getting it," Alex mumbled.

Danny patrolled the hallway, shoving a herd of Zeppelin fans into elevators. A tiny girl tried to slip past him and he lunged, snagging the back of her shirt and hurling her into the elevator. Now and then he barked orders into his broken walkie-talkie.

"HQ, this is Hall Patrol. We have a situation on twenty-one. Backup requested."

Alex worked on the door behind me.

"Got it," he whispered. "Going in."

Alex slipped into the room and closed the door behind him. This was it. Grab the money and get the fuck out. I glanced frantically back and forth from the door behind us to the door up the hall where Frenchy had disappeared with Richard. A few minutes later Alex popped his head out from the doorway.

"I can't find it, man. There's nothing here."

Danny walked toward us.

"All clear. Let's get this and go."

"It's not here, man. I can't find anything."

"You dumbass," Danny spit. "I'm going in."

Danny barged into the room, shoving Alex out of the way and banging the door against the wall as he hurled it open.

"Shit. Watch the hallway," I said to Alex.

He nodded and jogged off down the hallway.

I entered the room. Danny stood on the other side ripping empty drawers out of a long dresser and throwing them on the floor. The contents of Richard's luggage lay dumped in a pile next to an overturned nightstand.

"Where's the fucking money, asshole?" Danny snarled as I shut the door behind me.

"Relax. It's gotta be here."

"No. It's not. I've looked fucking everywhere."

"All right. Just calm down."

"Fuck you, Patrick," he heaved. "Are you guys trying to pull something on me?"

He stopped and glanced around the room.

"Wait," he muttered to himself. "Maybe there's a safe."

He knocked a painting off the wall over the TV and another from over the bed. Nothing.

"I ain't leaving here without that money," he shouted.

He spun toward me and pulled a small silver pistol from his waistband.

"All right," he said calmly. "New fucking plan."

"Whoa, Danny! Take it easy."

I backed up toward the door.

"Here's what we're doing. Me and you wait in the shower for this New York City asshole to return."

"I think he's actually British."

"*I don't give a shit!*" he screamed.

He hurled a drawer at the bed, where it bounced off the mattress and flipped onto the floor. His fist closed tight around the gun.

"When he comes back we stick him up and make him give us the money."

"No fucking way. I'm not doing it."

"Yes, you fucking are," Danny spoke slowly.

He held the gun at his side. Every muscle tightened as Danny erupted. He screamed and swung his arm wildly, sweeping everything on the dresser to the floor. He tore the curtains off the wall and hurled them at the TV. His eyes locked on the TV then turned to the window. I could read the thought from across the room. I had to stop him.

He lunged toward the TV and his foot hooked on an empty drawer and a pile of clothes, sending him stumbling into the corner of the bed. He fell face-first onto the mattress and bounced off onto the floor with a grunt. I watched from the other side of the bed for him to get up.

He rose with a scream. He squatted and grabbed the bottom of the bed with both hands and flipped it over. It spun, taking the nightstand with it in a tornado of pillows and paisley bedspread. My eye caught a silver glint in the air.

I dove onto my stomach and searched through the sheets. My fingertips hit cool metal and I wedged myself between the mattress and the wall to reach it. My fingers fumbled, burrowing through the sheets, until they pulled the object into the palm of my hand. Danny hurdled over the bed frame toward me, the gun tight in his fist. I shot my arm into the air, the metal key ring dangling on my finger. Danny stood over me and then lowered the gun as he read the tag:

SAFE DEPOSIT BOX 51.

NINETEEN
all access

the mad CRUSH OF PARTIERS IN THE LOBBY LOOKED AT MY HAND AND GOT THE FUCK OUT OF THE WAY. WE DIDN'T HAVE ANY TIME TO WASTE AND I KNEW WHEN I GRABBED THE ALL-ACCESS LED ZEPPELIN BACKSTAGE PASS FROM RICHARD'S LUGGAGE THAT THE SIGHT OF IT WOULD CAUSE THE CROWD TO PART. EVERY EYE FOLLOWED THE PASS AS ME AND DANNY BURST THROUGH THE LOBBY. A FEW FANS TRIED TO TALK TO US OR HIT US UP FOR TICKETS TO THE SHOW BUT I SHRUGGED THEM OFF WITH A LINE ABOUT "OFFICIAL ZEPPELIN BUSINESS."

The clerk at the front desk didn't look any happier than earlier. In fact, he looked worse. While we were upstairs, someone had dropped a bottle of red wine on the thick, cream-colored carpet and someone else had pissed in the back hallway. The clerk looked from me to Danny and back again, trying to put the pieces together. I held the backstage pass and the safe deposit box key up for him to see.

"I just need to get into our box," I said.

"Sir, typically we only allow the guest who requested the box to access it; in this case that would be Mr. Cole."

"Listen, Mr. Cole is in a meeting right now and he sent me down to pay the chauffeur for bringing our guitar back. Jesus, these guys. They get paid thousands to play the goddamn thing but can't remember to bring it with them."

He wasn't buying it. I jumped in before he could speak.

"You can call Richard if you'd like. He's in room twenty-one-ten."

This impressed the clerk and he dialed the number.

"Hello? Mr. Cole?"

Even from this side of the counter I could tell that Alex's British accent was bullshit. It sounded more Irish than anything, like a Lucky Charms cereal commercial. I had told him to keep it brief. He didn't.

"Would you like me to describe the chap I sent down?"

"No. That won't be necessary, sir."

"It's quite all right. He has long dark hair that needs a good washing. He's wearing jeans with a rip in the knee and a T-shirt with that horrible band Black Sabbath on it. No, wait, he's wearing a plain black T-shirt today."

"Okay, sir," the clerk said into the receiver.

"Now, if you could, be a mate and let him into the box. We need to pay off that arsehole of a chauffeur."

Red flooded into Danny's face as I choked back laughter. The clerk hung up and stared at the phone. He shook a set of keys over his head and walked toward the safe along the back wall. Danny and I followed.

Box number 51 sat at waist level on a wall of numbered boxes. I unlocked the box and Danny pulled it from the wall and lifted the lid. A few items lay scattered around inside: passports, receipts and a bundle of tickets for that night's show but not a single dollar.

"There's no fucking money in here," I said to Danny.

He stared into the box then slammed the lid closed and leapt around the vault stomping his feet and waving his arms in a silent temper tantrum until the gun fell down his pants leg and clattered across the tile floor. I put one finger to my lips, motioning for him to shut up.

"Everything all right in there, sir?" the clerk asked from outside the doorway.

"Sorry. We'll be right out," I answered.

I turned to Danny. His red face pulsed with his heavy breathing. I grabbed the bundle of tickets and stuffed them into my pocket.

"Let's go," I whispered. "We gotta get Alex and Frenchy and get out of here."

As we hurried across the hotel lobby I scanned the crowd for Richard Cole, a security guard or any other sign that someone was on to us. Something else stopped me cold: Emily. She stood across the lobby with Tina, Anna, Kyle and the rest of the Misty Mountain Hoppers. They lingered together near a couch in the back.

"This way!" I shouted, pulling Danny around a corner.

We shoved through a crowd of groupies and hurried down the hallway to the elevators. I pounded on the buttons. The numbers over the elevator door counted backward as the elevator crawled down from the twenty-first floor. I watched the lobby behind us for a sign that Emily or any of the Misty Mountain Hoppers were coming our way.

When the elevator doors opened, we tried to charge forward but ran into a wave of partiers getting off. A lanky kid in a flowered shirt and denim vest slumped in the corner. His bell-bottoms stretched out across the floor of the elevator.

"Let's go," I told the group. "Get him out of here."

A pair of scrawny hippies grabbed the kid's arm and tried

to yank him to his feet. They stumbled into each other and collided off the walls of the elevator. A small crowd formed outside the elevator.

"Wake up, man," I said, kicking his legs. "You gotta move."

His friends dropped his arms and stood in the middle of the elevator talking.

"Maybe if we all lift on the count of three?" the shortest one said.

Danny burst through them. He grabbed the kid's ankles and yanked. The force pulled the kid away from the wall and he slammed onto his back. His head ricocheted off the floor of the elevator and he groaned as Danny dragged him backward out of the elevator. Danny deposited him in the middle of the hallway and then shoved his way back onto the elevator.

"Let's go," he said as he jabbed at the elevator buttons.

Back on the twenty-first floor, Alex opened the door to Richard's room and we slipped in to return the key and backstage pass. Alex and I put the bed back together and shoved Richard's clothes back into his suitcase. The hallways were filling back up with groupies and hangers-on.

"Where's Frenchy?" I asked.

"He's still in there," Alex said, pointing down the hallway as we crept out of the room.

"I saw Tina and Emily in the lobby."

"What the fuck are they doing here?"

"They're with Emily's sister and the Misty Mountain Hoppers."

"Shit. How much did we get from the safe deposit box?"

"Nothing.

"Nothing? What are we gonna do?"

"We're getting the fuck out of here."

The look on his face confirmed the plan I'd already formed on the way up. Get Frenchy. Get out. If we were lucky, Jimmy

Page would pay Frenchy for the '58 Les Paul and we could escape from this mess with a few grand toward paying off Boogie. Maybe it would be enough. If we weren't lucky, we were all going to jail.

Someone needed to go to Page's room and pull Frenchy out of there. We argued over which one of us would do it. Danny wanted to do it but Alex and I both knew that was a horrible idea. Alex flat out refused to do it. That left me. I wiped the sweat off my palms and headed down the hallway.

big boss man

the bulging ARMS OF THE SECURITY GUARD STANDING OUTSIDE JIMMY PAGE'S ROOM DIDN'T SCARE ME. NOT THAT MUCH. OR THE FACT THAT HE LOOKED ABOUT THE SIZE OF A BALTIMORE COLTS' LINEMAN AS HE LEANED OVER AND STARED AT ME THROUGH SLANTED EYES SHOVED INTO A BALD HEAD WITH A BUSHY HANDLEBAR MUSTACHE. NO. I WAS SCARED OF THE WAY HE ADJUSTED HIS JACKET. EVERY FEW SECONDS HE ROLLED HIS SHOULDERS AND TURNED AT THE WAIST, WHICH MADE ME THINK HE WAS PROBABLY ADJUSTING A PISTOL HOLSTER SOMEWHERE UNDER HIS ARM.

He started talking even before I did.

"Get the fuck out of here."

"My friend's in there."

"No, he isn't."

Through the door I heard guitars jamming loudly. One started to solo, stumbled a bit on some low notes and then ripped up the neck. A few seconds later the song fell apart into laughter.

"His name's Frenchy, uh, Reginald. He's got a Fifty-eight Les Paul with him. Jimmy wanted to buy it."

He looked me over then decided I wasn't much of a threat. He was right. He poked his head around the door. I heard Frenchy's voice, then the door swung open.

I walked slowly into the room, stepping around a large piece of luggage and a guitar case. Richard lounged on the edge of the bed smoking a cigarette and talking on the telephone. Frenchy sat across from him in a chair tuning his Telecaster. Jimmy Page sat next to him.

Jimmy seemed small even with the extra padding of a button-up shirt and blazer. Curly black hair hung in his pale face as he hunched over a guitar. A long black cord snaked across the floor to a tiny amplifier. Guitar cases cluttered the floor and an acoustic guitar lay on the bed. He and Frenchy traded off solos. Frenchy sounded pretty fucking good.

The song stopped and Frenchy looked up.

"Oh, hey, man. Jimmy, this is my friend Patrick."

"Nice to meet you," he said.

I scanned the room for the briefcase that might have the cash.

"Uh, nice to meet you too."

I looked at Frenchy.

"Sorry, French . . . I mean Reginald, we gotta get going."

"Really? What's the rush?" he asked.

"Has Jimmy had a chance to look at the Les Paul?" I pushed things along. "We really have to get going."

"Okay. Let's take a look," Jimmy said.

Jimmy opened the case holding the '58 Les Paul and stared at it for a minute before picking it up and plugging it in.

Frenchy fiddled around with an old blues tune. The muddy chords screamed from the tiny amp. He turned to Jimmy while he played.

"I just learned this one."

"Jimmy Reed." Jimmy nodded. "Bloody brilliant guitar player."

He threw a solo over what Frenchy played. I couldn't believe it. We came to rob the band and Frenchy was jamming with them. Richard put a finger into his ear and screamed into the phone, "I don't know. We're hanging out at the hotel for now. Jimmy's looking at a guitar. *I said Jimmy might buy a guitar.* I don't know. Reginald Chamberlain. Really? You've never heard of him. He's big-time, man."

Frenchy and Jimmy played back and forth like that for a few minutes until the hotel door crashed open. Peter Grant barreled across the room. His presence filled the entire suite. The furniture seemed to shrink to get out of his way.

"What's all this then?" he asked Richard.

"Jimmy's buying a guitar."

"So who the fuck is this?" he asked, flipping a finger toward me.

Richard shrugged and muttered something about me being with Frenchy and the guitar. By now, the jam session had sputtered to a halt.

"Don't I know you, mate?" Peter asked me.

"I don't think so." I shrugged.

Peter stared at me. Jimmy, Frenchy and Richard chattered behind us. In that big, bald head Peter was trying to place where he knew me from. I signaled to Frenchy for us to get the hell out of there.

"Hey, Jimmy," Frenchy spoke up. "We gotta roll."

"You guys staying for the show tonight?" Jimmy asked, lighting a cigarette.

Frenchy looked up at me like a kid pleading for one more hour at the playground. I answered before he could.

"No, man, I wish we could but we've got to get back."

"Are you sure? I can get you sorted with tickets."

This time I didn't look at Frenchy.

"I wish we could. Can't tell you how much I wish we could but our ride is leaving. He has to work in the morning."

"But Patrick, didn't you—" Frenchy started to say.

"It's real cool of you to offer, Jimmy. Really cool. Come on, Reginald, we better get going."

Jimmy laid the Les Paul back in the case and crouched over it, staring for a second before shutting the lid. He leaned in the bathroom doorway and swilled from a bottle of Jack Daniel's while Frenchy fumbled to put his Telecaster away.

"You sure you want to sell this?" Jimmy asked Frenchy.

"Yeah. That's what I do. I try not to get attached to them, ya know? Love 'em and leave 'em, right?"

Frenchy laughed nervously.

They talked back and forth about the guitar with Jimmy nearly talking Frenchy out of selling it. These are so rare these days, aren't they? Can you believe how great a condition it's in? Are you sure you want to sell it? Jimmy practically begged Frenchy not to sell it. I thought it was going to work. Luckily, Frenchy held his ground. They settled on a price of two grand, just enough to pay off Boogie.

Unfortunately, getting paid for anything caused tension. It didn't matter what you were dealing with. Put two groups of men in a room with a bit of money and people get edgy.

It didn't help the tension in the room as I angled to get a look at the money. I shifted and slipped, trying to see where the cash was kept and how much was there. Peter sat at the edge of the bed. Jimmy and Richard stood in the corner with their backs turned toward us. Richard pulled a wad of bills from his pocket and counted them, then Jimmy bent over to open the nightstand drawer. I stepped around the corner of the bed to take a look.

"Where the hell do you think you're going?" Peter asked.

"I was just gonna grab the money for the guitar so we can get going."

He pointed across the room behind me.

"You just stay right fucking there," he said calmly.

See, we're in a bit of a hurry, I started to answer as I stepped back, then decided not to push him.

Finally, Jimmy crossed the room.

"Here you go, Reg," Jimmy said, handing Frenchy a thick wad of bills.

"Cool. Great meeting you, man," Frenchy said. "Thanks for letting me jam with you. Hope I wasn't too terrible."

"No, no, you were fucking spot on." Jimmy grinned.

I moved Frenchy toward the door. When we got there, he turned around.

"Sorry. Forgot my guitar," Frenchy said. He hurried back across the room and lifted the black guitar case.

I bolted into the hallway. Frenchy hurried along behind me, lugging his guitar. We found Alex and Danny by the elevators.

"Frenchy got us two grand for the Les Paul," I told Alex.

"Nice fucking work, man," Alex said, slapping Frenchy on the back.

We waited for the elevator. Alex punched the call button trying to bring it up faster. A pair of businessmen shared the ride down and looked at us nervously before getting off on the fifteenth floor. They must have sensed something that the rest of us didn't. We were ten floors from the lobby when the elevator shuddered to a halt and Danny held his gun to Frenchy's head.

TWENTY-ONE
going down

frencht) stared AT THE GUN JAMMED AGAINST HIS FOREHEAD AND DIDN'T BLINK. EVERYTHING HAD HAPPENED SO FAST. ME AND FRENCHY WERE TALKING ABOUT JIMMY PAGE WHEN DANNY SLAMMED THE ELEVATOR'S EMERGENCY STOP BUTTON, YANKED THE GUN FROM HIS PANTS AND GRABBED FRENCHY BY THE THROAT. I BACKED AWAY FROM DANNY. ALEX STARTED SHOUTING.

"What the fuck are you doing?"

Danny stared at Frenchy.

"Gimme the money."

Frenchy clenched his lips and shook his head. He clutched the guitar case against his chest and cowered behind it. Alex kept talking.

"Danny! Put the fucking gun away. Put it away right fucking now."

"Gimme the fucking money, Frenchy."

"We need this money to pay off Boogie," Alex said.

"I don't care."

"This is your fucking mess, Danny!" I yelled. "You do this and we'll tell Backwoods Billy you were the one who stole his safe."

"Won't matter. I'm taking this money and leaving town."

"Then I'll go to the DA," I said calmly. "He already came to see me. He'll have you arrested. You want to go back to jail?"

Danny stared hard at me like I'd just slapped him. He slowly moved the gun toward me. His eyes glazed over while he considered shooting me.

Alex saw his chance and charged at Danny. They tangled together as Alex grabbed Danny's arm and jerked it upward, pointing the pistol at the ceiling. Danny yanked at the gun and hurled them both backward. They bounced off the back wall. Danny tried to spin off but Alex pinned him to the side of the elevator.

I rushed at them as Danny bent Alex's arm backward. An arm shot wildly from the knot of limbs and the cold metal butt of the gun rocketed into my nose. The force knocked me to the floor. Tears clouded my eyes and I couldn't breathe. Blood trickled down my face and across my lips.

"You don't know who you're fucking with, boy," Danny grunted. "I told ya I studied with a Navy SEAL."

They staggered around the tiny elevator, locked together in a fight for the gun. Frenchy crawled around them using his guitar case as a shield as he inched toward the control panel and pounded on the buttons. The elevator jerked and shuddered and started toward the lobby.

The motion knocked Alex off balance. He swayed to the left and Danny knocked him to the ground with a wobbly kick. With his arm free, Danny waved the gun around the elevator. None of us moved. He leveled the pistol at Frenchy's head and talked between gasps for air.

"That's it, Frenchy. Give me the goddamn money."

His heavy breathing echoed in the elevator. Frenchy looked to me with wide eyes that begged for me to tell him what to do. I gave him a look that I hoped told him not to be stupid. He tugged the wad of bills out and held it up. Danny snatched it from Frenchy's hand and stuffed the cash in his pocket.

"No hard feelings, boys," he panted. "You understand. Now when this door opens, you guys go your way and I'll go mine. Don't do anything crazy."

Later I learned that hundreds of fans in the hotel lobby spotted our stalled elevator and figured it held Lep Zeppelin preparing for their grand exit out of the building. Word spread and people rushed toward the elevators. When the doors shuddered open, a mob of screaming groupies, drug-addled hippies, autograph collectors and weirdos crushed forward. Emily, Tina and the rest of the Misty Mountain Hoppers stood in the front. Emily screamed first.

"Oh my God! Patrick!"

I slumped against the back wall of the elevator holding both hands over my nose. A warm trickle of blood snaked down my arm and formed a small pool between my legs. Frenchy crouched in the corner behind his guitar case and Alex leaned against the wall, holding his stomach. He reached out for the wall to keep from falling over. Danny stood in the middle of the elevator and ignored us. He adjusted his tie then walked calmly through the crowd.

I pulled myself up and wobbled toward Emily. My legs felt like jelly. Frenchy crept sheepishly out of the elevator with his guitar and Alex limped behind him. The Misty Mountain Hoppers surrounded us.

"What happened to you guys? What is going on?" Emily asked, grasping my arm.

I started to answer then stopped. I didn't know what to say. Should I tell them that I just tried to rob their favorite band in the entire world? Should I admit that it didn't work and now I was caught between a funk band called the New York Giants and a born-again motorcycle gang called the Holy Ghosts and that either one of them might kill me? Should I say that the two grand that would have saved me was walking out the door in the hands of the man who got me into this fucking mess in the first place?

Then it hit me. It hit me like a pistol to the face. I stepped forward, cupped both hands around my mouth and screamed the one thing I could think of sure to cause utter fucking chaos in a swarm of crazed Zeppelin fans.

"That guy just robbed Led Zeppelin! Somebody stop him!"

Panic surged across the lobby. The army of dazed and drugged-out fans transformed into a seething mob. Beer bottles, cameras and backpacks crashed to the lobby floor as Zeppelin fans dropped everything and ran after Danny. Halfway across the hotel lobby, Danny stood frozen. He clutched his chauffeur's hat in his hands and backed toward the doors.

"I never robbed anybody! Hold on a minute. You guys don't know who you're fucking with!"

A wave of punches and kicks swallowed Danny. The chauffeur's hat hurled into the air. The sound of a body smacking onto the marble floor echoed through the lobby and someone screamed for the hotel clerk to call the police. Frenchy and I shoved through the crowd. Danny lay pinned on the lobby floor, his arms and legs restrained by screaming fans. Hands tore at him and a female hand held on to a mess of his hair. He craned his neck and our eyes met.

"Patrick! What the fuck? Get 'em off me!"

I jabbed my hand into Danny's pocket and palmed the wad of cash. His eyes narrowed.

"You motherfucker! You can't do this! Look, everyone—he has the money! Not me! It wasn't me!"

Frenchy leaned forward, cocked back a bony fist and punched Danny in the nuts. Danny howled. On the other side of the crowd, Emily ran toward me.

"What are you guys doing here? What happened?" she gasped.

"We drove up here so Frenchy could sell Jimmy Page a guitar."

"What? Really?"

A bell rang as the elevator doors opened behind us and I jerked my head to look back. Peter, Richard and a team of Zeppelin security stormed into the lobby. Peter's giant head swiveled, scanning the lobby.

"We gotta get out of here," Alex whispered to me.

"Listen, I gotta go. I'll call you and explain everything," I told Emily as I backed away.

She grabbed my arm.

"You can't leave! You have to talk to the police so they can arrest Danny. They're gonna want a report from you. He just robbed Led Zeppelin!"

Peter Grant bulldozed through the crowd with Zeppelin's security fanned out around him. Emily looked over her shoulder at Peter and Richard coming toward us. When she looked back at me her face had changed.

"I'm sorry," I said. "I gotta go."

Me, Alex and Frenchy hurried down the back hallway toward the kitchen, counting on it having an exit. Frenchy struggled to keep up as he lugged his heavy guitar case. Zeppelin security closed in on us. A swarm of fans and hotel employees passed us headed in the opposite direction. I pulled out the stack of concert tickets I stole from Zeppelin's safe deposit box and tossed them into the air.

"Free Zeppelin tickets!" I yelled.

Every face in the hallway stared upward as hundreds of tickets spun slowly toward the ground. Fans dove to the tile floor to gather tickets. Zeppelin security turned the corner and slammed into the crowd clamoring for tickets on the tile floor. Peter's arms waved wildly as he stumbled over someone and slammed into the wall.

Alex led us toward the kitchen door. A hand squeezed tightly on my arm before I could slip through.

"Hey—you work for Zeppelin," the hotel clerk said. "What the hell happened up there?"

I stared at him and blinked.

"He held us at gunpoint," I finally answered. "Then he brought me downstairs and forced me to empty the safe deposit box."

"I knew something was fishy when you came down," the clerk said. "It just didn't feel right."

"He's a dangerous man. I think he still has a gun on him."

"Don't worry. The police are pulling in now."

That wasn't good.

"Good," I said. "Now, is there any way you can find me a towel for my nose? It's finally stopped bleeding."

"Absolutely, Mr. . . . . I'm sorry, I didn't catch your name."

"It's John. John Osbourne," I said.

"I'll be right back, Mr. Osbourne," he said, disappearing down the hallway.

When he rounded the corner, I bolted from the back door in the kitchen and met up with Frenchy and Alex across the street. The crowd on Park Avenue swallowed us as we ran toward the garage two blocks over where we parked my car. A police car roared past us toward the hotel.

"What do you think will happen to Danny?" Alex asked as we climbed the concrete steps of the parking garage.

"He didn't actually rob Zeppelin so that'll be dropped," I said.

"But he did rob us."

"They'll have to drop that too since we aren't going to press charges."

"So they'll let him go?"

"Nah," I said. "He still violated his parole. Plus he's carrying a gun. He's gonna be fucked."

Frenchy hadn't said a word. He walked ahead of me and Alex with his head down. The black guitar case knocked against his leg as he trudged across the parking garage. Me and Alex looked at each other and both thought the same thing. Frenchy was hiding something. He never could keep a secret.

"What's going on, Frenchy?"

"Well . . ." He hesitated. He pointed at the guitar case. "I stole one of Jimmy's guitars."

"How the hell did you do that?" Alex asked.

He really sounded impressed.

"When me and Patrick were leaving I went back to grab my Telecaster but I took this case instead. I don't know what came over me. I figured, whatever's in this case has to be better than my shitty Fender."

"What were you going to do if he caught you?" Alex asked.

"All the cases looked the same anyway so if he stopped me I figured I'd just play dumb and act like it was a mistake."

"Our little Frenchy has become a real thief," I said, grinning.

"You sly fucking dog." Alex grinned too.

"Let's take a look," I said.

Frenchy leaned the guitar case upright against the bumper of my car. The snap of the clasps opening echoed across the empty concrete garage. He swung the lid open and cash flooded out onto the greasy garage floor in thick bundles.

Wads of twenties, fifties and hundreds bounced across the concrete.

"Holy fuck!" Alex screamed.

He jumped up and down, waving his arms, then ran a giant circle around the empty parking garage, screaming.

Frenchy stood frozen with his mouth hanging up.

Me and Alex grabbed the case and began shoveling the money back inside. Frenchy still hadn't moved.

"How much you think is here?" Alex asked.

"I'm guessing about fifty thousand."

"No way. There's gotta be at least a hundred grand."

"You're crazy. There's no way it's that much."

It took Alex and Frenchy most of the three-hour drive home to count all $203,000.

We were both wrong.

TWENTY-TWO

the green, green grass of home

A voice YELLED FROM THE OTHER SIDE OF A THICK WOODEN DOOR, "WHO THE FUCK IS IT?"

"Boogie! It's me, Patrick."

Loud music thumped inside the house. Boogie asked again. This time I shouted.

"Boogie! It's Patrick and Alex! We're here about the safe!"

One eye peered through the tiny curtained window then Boogie jerked the door open. The force nearly tore it off the rusted hinges. He motioned us inside.

"Shit, man. Keep it down," he said, leaning out and looking up and down the street. "It's late and my neighbors are some nosy motherfuckers."

It took us half an hour of driving around in the dark to find Boogie's house again. We were exhausted. Nerves in the car were seriously frayed after everything that went down at the Drake Hotel followed by three hours of major freaking out in the car while Frenchy and Alex counted the money.

We argued most of the time about whether we were or weren't going to get arrested, why we should or shouldn't return the money or whether Alex should buy a Mustang or a Nova with his share of the cash.

We dropped the cash at Frenchy's house, figuring it to be the safest place. Then we drove in circles trying to remember where Boogie lived. We needed to pick up the safe. I wouldn't be able to sleep until I paid Boogie and loaded the safe into the car. I didn't give a damn how late it was when we got there.

Turns out, Boogie was having a small party and his place thundered with loud funk music and laughter. Johnny Paycheck danced in the middle of the living room with a tall black girl who, even without her huge platform shoes, would have towered over him. Bleary-eyed partiers sat in a row on the sofa, passing a series of bongs laid out on the coffee table next to a brick of weed and a pistol. The coffee table looked familiar.

"Is that our safe?" I asked Boogie, nearly screaming to be heard over the music.

"Yeah. Yeah. That's it right there."

He turned the music down as he passed the stereo. A skinny guy stretched his long legs across the top of the safe and Boogie slapped his feet to the ground as he walked over.

"Get up, motherfuckers. We gotta move this shit."

The stoner crew on the couch grumbled and shifted in their seats but no one really moved until Boogie leaned in and slapped one of them upside the head. The entire crew then scurried to get away from him.

"Where you going? Get your asses over here and help with this."

With the bongs, weed and weapon cleared off the top I could see the safe laid on its back in the middle of the living room. The door had been replaced and the chipped-up dial from the old safe had been fitted into the new lock. It looked good. With a little help, Boogie groaned and set it upright.

"Are the tapes inside?" I asked him.

"Yeah. I think so. You wanna check?"

"Yeah. What's the combination?"

"Damn," he said, shaking his head. "I knew you were going to ask me that. Let me find it."

Boogie emptied his pockets onto the top of a giant stereo speaker—a wad of bills, a giant switchblade, a pair of guitar picks, a packet of cocaine and a few stray bullets.

"Shit, Johnny. Where did we put the combo to that motherfucker?"

"Hell, I don't know," Paycheck said, leaning into his girl.

"Quit fucking around. Where is it?"

Paycheck dug through his back pocket then handed Boogie a scrap from a cardboard Budweiser box with numbers scrawled on it. Boogie opened the safe. The two tapes sat on the bottom shelf.

"There you go, man. Just like I promised. You got the money?"

Alex put his hand on my shoulder and looked around the party. He was right. Handing Boogie two grand in the middle of a party made me nervous.

"You ain't gotta worry about these idiots." Boogie grinned.

He lifted the front of his T-shirt and showed us a pistol jutting from his waistband.

I struggled to pull the fat wedge of cash from my front pocket then slipped it to Boogie. He looked around the living room then snuck off to the kitchen to count the money. He might not have been nervous for me to hand off the money in front of his friends, but he sure didn't want to flash it around them. He returned a few minutes later, smiling, and shouted to Johnny Paycheck, "Yo, Johnny! It's cool!"

"We're all cool?"

They high-fived and laughed loudly.

"Ah yeah! We're getting that Moog tomorrow. Hot damn!"

Johnny Paycheck danced across the room then threw his arm around Alex's neck.

"You all want a beer?"

He brought me, Alex and Frenchy each a can of beer. We stood against the wall and drank them and tried not to look like the only three white guys in the house. A pack of girls danced in the middle of the room but we were all too nervous to walk over. Alex got stoned with a few guys then grabbed more beers for us from the fridge. Soon I was drunk and arguing with Boogie.

"I'm just saying Sly Stone is overrated."

"Overrated! You're out of your fucking mind. The guy invented funk all by himself," Boogie shouted, leaning over. His bushy Afro poked into my face.

I shrugged. That made him madder.

" 'Dance to the Music.' You're gonna tell me you don't like 'Dance to the Music'?"

I shrugged again and sipped my beer.

"Ah, man. You don't know shit, white boy." He laughed.

As the party wound down, me, Alex and Frenchy sat around

the safe in the living room. Boogie nodded off in a recliner. Over by the stereo, Johnny searched through the eight-tracks for some music.

"All you have is loud-ass funk. Where is the after-party music, Boogie?"

Boogie sat up and shrugged, his eyes glazed with beer and pot.

"You ain't got any Bobby Blue Bland? What about Otis, man? Where's the Otis?"

Johnny Paycheck scattered a pile of eight-track tapes then flipped through a crate of records. When he didn't find anything he liked, he grunted and walked away. He swayed a bit in the middle of the room then steadied himself on the edge of the safe.

"What's in this motherfucker?" he said, leaning over and spilling his beer on the carpet. He swung open the door to the safe.

"Aw, damn," he said. "Jim Nabors. Let's put this shit on."

"No, no, no," I said. "We gotta give that back to Backwoods Billy."

"Damn, man," Johnny Paycheck taunted me. "It won't hurt it. We got the reel-to-reel right here!"

He held the tapes up over my head and out of reach. I gave up.

"Just let me hear 'Green, Green Grass of Home.' You know that tune? This guy thinks he's coming home but really he wakes up and he's in prison and he's been dreaming. That song is badass."

He loaded the reels into Boogie's player. The machine hissed and clicked as the tape set up. He cranked the volume and pressed *play*. Through the static a voice spoke loudly in the speakers.

"... it's the same every month. It's not, uh, up for negotiation. A thousand dollars' cash, two hundred Black Beauties, two hundred Blue Devils, a pound of weed and whatever Percocet you dirtbags have around. That's the price you pay for my, uh, assistance."

My heart rocketed up into my throat. I knew that voice.

"Now where am I gonna get Percocet, Cooper? I ain't no fucking doctor."

I knew that voice too.

TWENTY-THREE

let's make a deal

my dirty CHUCK TAYLORS SQUEAKED ACROSS THE MARBLE FLOOR IN THE COURTHOUSE. THE SOUND ECHOED AROUND THE HIGH CEILING CAUSING EVERYONE TO STARE. FUCK IT, I THOUGHT. THEY WOULD HAVE STARED ANYWAY. IT'S NOT OFTEN YOU SEE A KID WITH LONG HAIR AND A BLACK SABBATH SHIRT STROLLING THROUGH THE COURTHOUSE. NOT UNLESS HE'S WEARING HANDCUFFS.

The security guard towered over the desk at the elevator. His starched uniform dangled off his bony shoulders as if he were a scarecrow. He slicked back his silver hair and chomped nervously on a toothpick when he saw me. He stuck out a thin hand as I walked past the desk.

"Wait a second. Where you going, bud?"

I leaned over the desk.

"I have an appointment on the fourth floor."

"With who?"

"Simon Cooper. District Attorney."

He pointed to the tapes under my arm.

"If that's a delivery you gotta take the service elevator round back."

"Special delivery." I smiled, eating a mint out of a bowl on his desk. "He's expecting me."

His eyes lingered on me then he picked up the phone.

"This is the security desk," he said. "I got a young man here says he's here to see Mr. Cooper . . . Oh really . . . I understand . . . Yes, I'll escort him."

He hung up the phone then grabbed a large ring of keys from the desk.

"Let's go," he grunted.

"It's all right. I can find it on my own," I said as I followed him down the wide marble hallway.

"They want me to escort you."

"What do they think I'm going to do, steal something?" I laughed.

"Nope. They told me to make sure you and that delivery get there right away."

The guard trudged on ahead of me. Cooper's office sat at the end of a long, wood-paneled hallway. The frosted-glass door led to a waiting room where a stubby secretary typed behind an oversized desk.

"He's all yours," the guard said before he left.

She looked up at me then at the boxes under my arm.

"You can just leave those here on the desk, young man," she said. "I'll make sure Mr. Cooper gets them."

I smiled and sat down on a deep leather couch along one wall. She looked up from her typewriter then picked up a phone and whispered.

A few minutes later Cooper leaned in the doorway to his office. He straightened his tie then rubbed his three-day beard. Dark circles surrounded his eyes and his face seemed pale. He looked like he hadn't left his office in days. He still had his pricey suit and greasy smirk, though, all the signs of a privileged fuck-up who found ways to con others into cleaning up his mistakes. Someone who counted on his charm and money to make up for all of the trouble he got into. Right now he was counting on that charisma to con me into handing over the tapes I held under my arm. It wouldn't be that easy.

"Patrick!" He grinned. "Come on in. No calls please, Joyce."

Cooper's office looked like the den of a man trying to hold down a serious job while juggling an even more serious drug habit. Sunlight wrestled through the closed blinds and curtains. Piles of papers lined the floor along the walls, most likely put there during a speed-induced effort to get organized. The products from all his late nights cluttered the top of a filing cabinet—deodorant, eye drops, two unopened dress shirts, an iron, several toothbrushes and a collection of pill bottles.

He closed the door behind us then stood in the middle of the office looking me over.

"Good to see you." He grinned. "I was worried. I've looked just about everywhere for you. You're a hard guy to find."

"I had a few things to take care of out of town." I shrugged.

"Well, here you are. This is good. This is really good. Sorry about this mess."

"Looks like you've been busy."

"The mayor isn't too happy about the hell Backwoods Billy and his buddies raised down at the Inner Harbor. Those boneheads put thirteen carnies in the hospital. The mayor wants somebody to answer for it."

I shifted the tapes under my arm and asked a stupid question.

"So Backwoods Billy is in jail?"

"Nah." Cooper fidgeted. "They've got nothing on him. Can't

even prove he was involved. I've been holed up in here dealing with all the arrests."

He twirled an expensive-looking cuff link and lost himself in thought then quickly shook it off.

"Anyway, Patrick, what's new?"

I held up the tapes. A pained grin crept across his face.

"Find those in Billy's safe?"

I nodded.

"I figured that was why you called me. I knew you'd come through for me. Did you listen to them?"

"Yeah. Pretty interesting stuff."

He hung on to the dopey grin and nodded. Nothing shook this guy.

"I bet."

"Drugs, prostitutes, payoffs." I whistled loudly. "There's even a conversation on here where someone who sounds just like you talks about putting a hit out on a lawyer. Now, you're a DA. Is that a felony or a misdemeanor? I think it's a felony, but you're the expert."

The grin dissolved. He lit a cigarette and waved the smoke out of his face.

"Do you know who made these tapes?" I asked.

"I have an idea." He grimaced.

"Yeah? How did it happen?"

"I was going through a rough time and some scumbags I thought were my friends decided to take advantage of me."

"Here's what I think happened," I said. "You worked out a deal with Backwoods Billy where he'd set you up every month with pills, drugs, a bit of cash and whatever else you wanted. In exchange, you'd make any legal messes involving the Holy Ghosts disappear. Is that right?"

He crossed his arms and stared at me.

"Like I said, I was going through a rough time."

"You thought Backwoods Billy was some dumb hillbilly, right? Then he taped his conversations with you, cut off the payments and made you help the Holy Ghosts anyway."

Cooper shrugged and gave me a look like I'd just told him the most obvious fact in the world.

"Then the cops arrested the Holy Ghosts for beating the living shit out of me at the carnival and one of the cops mentions something about me having their safe. You thought you could use me to get the tapes back because I wouldn't know what they were and how much they were worth around here."

He stubbed out his cigarette.

"And right now I bet Backwoods Billy is threatening you with these tapes unless you make this Inner Harbor mess go away. That's why you've been holed up in here trying to track me down. And I know he's out there looking for me. He needs the tapes to make all this trouble go away and you need the tapes to make him go away."

Cooper shuffled around his desk. He sat down in the cushy leather chair and unlocked a drawer then removed a few bottles of pills, some tiny vodka bottles and a thick roll of cash.

"Let's get to it, Patrick. How much do you want?"

"I want my friend Keith released from jail. All charges dropped."

"You mean your idiot friend that the cops arrested during the brawl?" he scoffed. "You know, he's suspected of stealing a very rare and expensive guitar from Haven Street Pawnshop. Hell, between you and me, you're a suspect too."

"No, I'm not," I said, tapping the tapes.

Cooper tugged at his messy hair then groaned loudly.

"Fine. Is that it?"

I smiled.

"That's it. Just do your job."

"My job is putting people away. Not getting them off."

"Good," I said. "You can start by locking up Backwoods Billy and the Holy Ghosts. I don't want to live the rest of my life hiding under a table every time I hear a motorcycle."

"Don't worry. I'll take care of it."

"Give it until tomorrow. I want to go see Backwoods Billy tonight."

"Don't be an asshole, kid. Let it go."

Cooper stood up and walked around his desk. He smoothed his tie and fidgeted.

"So we have a deal?"

"One more thing," I said. "I'm keeping a copy of the tapes for myself just in case you don't hold up your end of the bargain."

"I figured."

I tossed the tapes on Cooper's desk.

"I'll pick Keith up tonight at five. Make sure he's ready."

Cooper nodded. He sat on the edge of his desk holding the reels in his hands. Something hit me as I walked to the door. I had to ask.

"You know anything about a guy named Danny Carter? Guy from around here who was arrested in New York over the weekend with a gun? Something about him and Led Zeppelin?"

"Yeah. I heard about that. Parole violation. Weapons possession."

"How long you think he'll go away for?"

"Probably another five. Why? You want him out too? 'Cause that's one even I don't think I can save."

I thought for a second. Just a second.

"Nah. You can have him."

TWENTY-FOUR

getting away with murder

"this place IS FUCKED," ALEX SAID AS WE CROSSED THE PARKING LOT BEHIND SHOOTERS BAR, THE UNOFFICIAL CLUBHOUSE OF THE HOLY GHOSTS.

I called the bar earlier in the day and promised Backwoods Billy we'd be there later to drop off the safe. Alex and Frenchy came with me. As we pulled into the gravel parking lot I wondered how many poor suckers were led into the dark woods behind Shooters and never seen again. Frenchy thought the same thing.

"We're gonna be buried out here." He sighed.

Inside Shooters, Backwoods Billy stood by the pool table, holding a cue in one hand and glass of whiskey in the other.

He wore a blue bandanna tied around his head covering a white bandage. A black leather vest hung over his plain gray tank top.

"It's your shot, Billy," Rabbit said to him as we walked in.

The stools and tables sat empty except for a few Holy Ghosts lounging around the pool table. The rest of the gang was still locked up in jail. Billy bent over the table. His sunglasses fell off the top of his head and rolled across the green felt. Everyone laughed. Billy grinned then dropped his cue on the tile floor. He was drunk.

"Boys! Come on in." He waved to us.

We slunk into the bar and stood behind a row of stools loaded with Holy Ghosts. I recognized the pockmarked face of a kid at the end of the row as the guy Alex pummeled at the Inner Harbor. A tan bandage covered his nose. He looked younger than I'd remembered. The chubby guy standing next to him raised his bald head to look us over, then grinned. He pointed at Alex.

"Hey! That's the kid that whipped Sonny's ass at the carnival."

Everyone laughed except Sonny.

"Fuck you, Whitey," Sonny mumbled.

"I'm telling ya, that boy can duke," Whitey said. "What's your name, kid?"

"Alex."

"Don't mess with this kid, boys. He's a fucking animal."

Alex lit a cigarette to keep from looking nervous.

Backwoods Billy took his shot. The cue ball missed the three ball by about a foot, bounced off the bumper, crossed the middle of the table and sunk the eight ball in the corner.

"Well, shit." He laughed. "I just fucking blew that."

He set the cue back in the rack on the wall then walked toward me.

"Come here, Patrick," he said, motioning toward the bar. "Let's talk."

Rabbit racked the pool balls as we walked away. He asked if anybody wanted to play.

"I do!" I heard Frenchy say.

I sat on a bar stool next to Backwoods Billy. He leaned over the bar, pulled a bottle of beer from a tub of ice and handed it to me.

"You did a good thing bringing that safe back, boy."

"Thanks," I stammered.

"Listen to me, Patrick. You did the right thing by fixing this mess before it got out of hand."

I looked up at the bandage peeking out beneath the bandanna on his head. He caught me staring.

"Don't worry about this," he said, running his finger over the bandage. "It happens. Comes with the turf, kid. Shit, I've been beaten worse and left for dead. Besides, you shoulda seen what was left of them carnies. It weren't pretty."

"So we're cool?"

"We're cool, kid. Don't worry. Remember: 'If thy brother trespasses against thee, rebuke him; and if he repents, forgive him.' You know where that's from?"

I didn't know jackshit about the Bible but for some reason I felt pressured to take a guess. I tried the only two names I knew other than Jesus.

"Is that Luke or something? Maybe John?"

"Well, all right, boy. Luke 17:3. Guess you've been reading that Bible I gave ya. I am impressed. Let's have a shot."

A chubby lady in a sleeveless David Allan Coe T-shirt shuffled behind the bar. Backwoods Billy motioned for her and she set out a row of shot glasses. Backwoods Billy grabbed the bottle of tequila and lifted it over his head.

"Who wants a shot of tequila?"

A few of the Holy Ghosts wandered over. Sonny stayed on his stool.

"What's the matter, Sonny?" Billy yelled. "Your pussy hurt or something?"

Everyone laughed. Rabbit yelled from the other side of the bar. He pointed at Frenchy.

"Billy, get this kid a shot."

"You're just trying to get him drunk 'cause he's beatin' you." Whitey laughed.

"Goddamn right. He's whipping my ass."

"What have I told you about using the Lord's name in vain, Rabbit?"

"Sorry, Billy."

We came together and Backwoods Billy poured a round of tall tequila shots then passed them to us. We raised our glasses.

"All right, boys. Here's to staying free!"

We all shouted, "Amen."

The warm tequila burned down my throat.

Backwoods Billy sent Whitey, Sonny and some of the other Holy Ghosts to haul the safe into the bar. They struggled, sweating and grunting, as they plowed through the door. The safe landed with a heavy thud on the floor by a back table. He never told them what it was or where it came from. They never asked.

I kept one eye on Backwoods Billy. If he had any sense he'd check for the tapes in the safe before letting me go. He played it cool for a while then he handed me some change and asked me to play some music on the jukebox. While I stood flipping through the Merle Haggard and Hank Williams Jr. records on the jukebox, Backwoods Billy squatted in front of the safe and dialed the combination. The door unlocked flawlessly and he peeked inside. Satisfied with seeing the tapes in their boxes on the shelf, he called me over for another shot.

Whitey, Sonny, Backwoods Billy and a few other Holy Ghosts stood around the bar drinking and talking about the fight at the Inner Harbor. Someone bragged about breaking a whiskey bottle over a carny's head and Sonny claimed to have smashed someone's nose with brass knuckles. They laughed a lot, even if they were on the losing end of a pool cue or baseball bat in the story. I clutched the beer bottle in my hand. Backwoods Billy slurred in my ear, "You know, that boy Alex of yours would make a good Holy Ghost. I ain't bullshitting. That boy can fight."

I didn't know what to say.

"He ever ridden a motorcycle?" he asked me.

Before I could answer, a wooden snap rang out by the pool table. Rabbit stood with a broken pool cue in his hand. He glared at Frenchy. Alex stood between them with his arms up, asking Rabbit to calm down. At six-foot-something and about 250 pounds, Rabbit could tear Frenchy in half. There was nothing Alex could do about it. Rabbit's chest heaved and he clutched a broken half of a pool cue in each meaty fist.

There are a few rules to remember when hanging around a motorcycle gang. Never get drunk with them because they will end up kicking the shit out of you. When one of them does finally kick the shit out of you, everyone else in the room will help. And most important, never, ever under any circumstance touch, insult or otherwise disrespect the gang or a gang member's jacket. That'll get you killed.

Those rules were the farthest thing from Frenchy's mind as he stood on the other side of the table. His sweaty hair flopped around his face and he blinked nervously behind his thick glasses. In his arms he held a death sentence—Rabbit's leather jacket and denim vest. The Holy Ghosts patch wrinkled in his tight grip.

"Whoa, boys!" Backwoods Billy yelled. "What the hell's going on?"

"That boy just took my colors!" Rabbit yelled.

"You better put that down, son," Backwoods Billy said to Frenchy. "Touching a man's colors can get your fucking skull split."

"I won it. Fair and square."

Backwoods Billy turned to Rabbit, his face pulsating with rage.

"You bet your fucking colors on a pool game?"

"He said he wanted to bet my colors against his fifty grand!" Rabbit explained. "I thought it was a joke! Where's a kid like that gonna get fifty grand?"

Goddamn it, Frenchy.

I stepped forward before Frenchy could talk.

"He was just joking! Everybody calm down. Let's relax. No more pool. Okay, Frenchy?"

I took the pool cue out of his hand. Frenchy started to say something until I glared at him. Alex pried the jacket from his hands and dropped it on the pool table. The jacket fell with a thud on the green felt.

"Maybe you boys don't fucking get it," Billy slurred loudly. "Those colors are not to be fucked with. We've killed guys just for disrespecting 'em."

The crowd of Holy Ghosts surrounded us in a tight circle.

"Maybe we should go?" I said. "My buddy is obviously a bit drunk."

"I'm not drunk," Frenchy protested.

"Yes, you are," Alex said.

He grabbed Frenchy's arm and walked him toward the door. Backwoods Billy stood in the middle of the bar thinking.

He swayed a bit and mumbled to himself about honor and God. Any second I expected him to give the order for the remaining Holy Ghosts to tear us apart. I pulled a fifty-dollar bill from my pocket and handed it to him.

"Here. I want to buy you guys some drinks. You know, as a way of saying I'm sorry for the way my friend acted."

Billy held the bill up and stared at it. Then he smiled.

"Well, that's mighty fine of you, Patrick. Listen, you boys are welcome here any time."

If I was lucky enough to get out of there alive once, I sure wasn't coming back.

"Thanks, Billy."

"God bless," he said as I walked away.

The last I saw of him he stood in the glow of the Budweiser light over the pool table, bandanna over his bandage, waving one arm wildly while preaching to a crowd of dirty bikers with their heads bent down. The safe sat, discarded, in the corner.

"You didn't have to buy that old bastard a drink," Alex said as we pulled out of the parking lot.

"I can afford it," I grinned. "Besides, it might be his last one for a long fucking time."

every day comes and goes

there's only SO MUCH *HAWAII FIVE-O* A MAN CAN WATCH. KEITH LOOKED LIKE HE'D HIT HIS LIMIT AND CRACKED A BIG GRIN THAT AFTERNOON AS HE WALKED THROUGH THE METAL DOOR AND INTO THE DISCHARGE AREA OF BALTIMORE COUNTY JAIL. HE WORE THE CLOTHES HE HAD ON WHEN THEY ARRESTED HIM: A RATTY BLACK T-SHIRT AND DIRTY JEANS, ONLY NOW THE JEANS SPORTED A GIANT STAIN IN THE FRONT.

"What happened to your jeans, Keith?" Alex asked as he opened the car door to let Keith into the backseat.

"I guess I must have pissed myself when they busted me," Keith shrugged. He stared at the stain for a second. "That just sucks."

Not even a piss stain could ruin Keith's mood. He glowed in the backseat of my car as we pulled away even if he couldn't figure out why they'd let him go.

While I drove to Frenchy's, Alex filled Keith in on everything that went down while he was locked up. The trip to

New York, the empty safe deposit box, Danny pulling the gun and our getaway. We didn't mention the money.

Frenchy sat in his basement playing guitar. He'd bought a case of beer and a pizza for Keith's welcome-home bash. We wanted to keep it low-key. Frenchy hugged Keith and handed him a bottle of Miller High Life and we all squeezed onto the tattered couch to eat. Neil Young's *Everybody Knows This Is Nowhere* played on the turntable.

"Shit, man," Keith said between bites. "Not to be a dick but you guys could have thrown a better party than this. This sorta sucks. Alex got a big-ass bash with chicks and everything. I got pizza, High Life and some Canadian asshole singing about a river or something."

"Next time, serve eight months instead of three days," Alex joked. "Besides, we got a surprise for you."

Keith jumped up from the couch.

"Holy shit! I knew it. You hired strippers! I fucking love you guys."

"Keith! Pay attention. This is important. And you can't tell anyone. Got it?"

"Yeah." Keith nodded.

"I'm serious. You cannot tell anyone. Not one single person."

Keith realized Alex was serious. He dropped back down onto the couch then bit into another piece of pizza.

"Keith. Look at me and tell me you won't say anything about this to anyone."

"Fuck. All right. I won't tell anyone."

"Go ahead and show him, Frenchy," I said.

Frenchy ran up the basement stairs and locked the door. The last thing we needed was his mom seeing the money. He came back, crouched on his knees and pulled the guitar case out from under his sofa. A steel chain rattled beneath the sofa and the guitar case jerked to a halt.

"Oops," Frenchy said. "Forgot I chained it up."

He fished a small key out of his pocket then unlocked the padlock and lugged the case to the middle of the room. We all stared at the case as Frenchy lifted the lid. I'd seen the pile of cash a dozen times and it still made my heart pound. This time I watched Keith's reaction. It hit him slowly then his eyes bugged out and he leapt off the couch.

"Oh my God! Holy shit! How much is there?"

"Two hundred thousand," I said.

"Where did you guys get that? You told me you didn't get nothing off Zeppelin."

"We didn't. Frenchy did. He thought he was stealing one of Jimmy's guitars. Turns out he hit the motherload."

"Shit, man. You guys are fucking rich."

Alex threw his arm around Keith.

"No, man. We're all rich. We're each taking fifty thousand. That includes you."

"Me? What the fuck did I do? I wasn't even there."

"You helped," I said. "We couldn't have gotten into Jimmy Page's room without that Les Paul. You helped us get it."

"And besides," Frenchy added, "if you hadn't been busted that night at the carnival the rest of us might not have gotten away."

"You guys are the fucking best," Keith said, hugging each of us.

We spent the rest of the night getting drunk and stoned and talking about what we were going to buy. Everything from El Caminos to rare comic books to a pet Chihuahua. Keith talked about wanting to play the stock market. He just had to figure out what it was first.

A few days later the cops raided Indian Winds trailer park. Real SWAT-team military-style. They came in early, kicked open trailer doors and caught most of the gang asleep next to their old ladies. Every Holy Ghost went down. Backwoods Billy, Rabbit, Whitey, Sonny and a paddy wagon full of others. The papers said the cops found barrels of pills and an arsenal filled with everything from AK-47s to tear-gas grenades. They also confiscated a crate of Bibles.

Backwoods Billy went nuts. Tore up two holding cells and an interrogation room before they calmed him down. He couldn't figure what went wrong and how his protection fell through. He left Cooper a streak of threats about releasing the tapes. Finally, he got wise and called his wife. She loaded the tapes into their reel-to-reel player and found what I'd recorded over them. I hope she liked Black Sabbath.

They sent Backwoods Billy to the same joint as Danny. The Maryland authorities dragged Danny back from New York and charged him with felony weapons possession and a parole violation. They dropped the robbery charges when they couldn't prove he stole anything from Led Zeppelin. The judge gave him five years. He'd be out in two.

Every newspaper in New York ran a major story on Led Zeppelin being ripped off. The headline read LED ZEPPELIN ROBBED OF 203G. The band stayed in New York an extra day to deal with everything and Zeppelin's manager held a press conference. They even called in the FBI.

The investigation went nowhere, probably because the band insisted the money was stolen from the safe deposit box. I couldn't figure out why they didn't tell the cops the cash was really in Jimmy's guitar case. It made sense later when I read about Zeppelin suing the hotel and winning a settlement.

My luck in Maryland was running out. I could feel it. And I knew a few of the lesser Holy Ghosts would be back on the street soon. I didn't want to be around when it happened. I went back to New York City. The new punk rock bands like the Ramones, the Dead Boys and the New York Dolls were taking off. I bought a nice camera with part of the money and took a few photos. Frenchy started a band. They weren't very good but now and then they played New York City.

Emily visited a lot. She was saving money and planned to move to New York City and take classes at NYU. She wanted to be a lawyer, just in case I ever needed one. I thought that was a great idea.

I didn't think about the robbery much. Just sort of pushed it to the back of my mind until one day, when I was shopping at a record store in the Village. Led Zeppelin's "Whole Lotta Love" played on the stereo. An older black man with a stack of blues records under his arm walked up to the counter.

"What the heck is this noise?" he asked, pointing toward the turntable. "What you need to do is play the originals."

"What do you mean?" the young clerk mumbled. He sounded incredibly stoned.

"The guys that Zeppelin stole these songs from. You know, Willie Dixon, Sleepy John Estes, Howlin' Wolf, Bukka White . . ."

"I don't know what you're talking about, buddy. This is Zeppelin."

The old man sighed. He'd obviously gone over this before.

"Someday, somebody's gonna clean these British boys out for what they've done," he said. Then he was gone.

I grinned and walked toward the register, Black Sabbath's new album under my arm and a fat wad of cash in my hand.

acknowledgments

Thanks to:

My girl Mel Gorski for understanding all those late nights of loud music, clanging beer bottles, and being woken up at 4 a.m. to be asked, "Does this suck?" I love you madly.

Tammy Buhrmester for tolerating decades of my ramblings, tantrums, craziness and "weird" music.

Ryan Lodge for creating so many of the riduculous situations in this dumb little book and for being my brother forever.

Kevin White for damn near everything. But mostly for understanding the utter fucking importance of Metallica.

Jesse Howard for all the shit talking and Wild Turkey. You're proof that nice boys really don't play rock 'n' roll.

Raquel Lauren and Bradley Peterson for that one perfect trip to Coney Island in a '71 Dodge.

And, of course, Nico for sitting on my lap the entire time and being the original black dog. You're the best friend a guy could ever ask for.

Special thanks to Matt "Kid Legs" Render, Kevin Schulz, Erik "Dry Gulch" Byrne, "Lil" Kenny Coulman, Rob Loudon, Wil "I'm Damaged" O'Neal, Zach Medearis, Matt Bertz, Ben Poskins, Alex "Axe Man" Luna, Bryan Joseph, and anyone else who's lunatic behavior may have found its way into these pages somehow. You all need professional help.

about the author

JASON BUHRMESTER was born in Kankakee, Illinois, which was voted the "Worst City in North America" by *The Places Rated Almanac*. Jason started his writing career in the customer service department at *Playboy* magazine and has since contributed to *Playboy, Maxim, Spin, Village Voice, Wired, Giant, FHM, Penthouse* and other publications. He is currently editor at *Inked* magazine and lives in Brooklyn with his wife, Melissa, and black pug, Nico. He feels that "Sabbath Bloody Sabbath" is Black Sabbath's best song. Visit jasonbuhrmester.com to disagree with him.